THOLOCCO'S
WAKE

THEOLOGO'S
WATCH

THOLOCCO'S WAKE

Book One of the Legacy Series

———◆———

W. W. Van Overbeke

atmosphere press

Published by Atmosphere Press

Cover design by

atmospherepress.com

TABLE OF CONTENTS

*For Beverley Bertholf
and Roland Gary*

EAGLE LAKE

Chapter One

July 19, 1968—Eagle Lake, Minnesota

"I should have divorced that son of a bitch years ago!"

Whenever Emma thought about her husband, she uttered these words. Though they had been separated now for fifteen years, her anger—and pain—was still very raw.

As she stood staring out her bedroom window, she noticed how the morning sun had already crested the Norway pines lining the road. The window was open a crack, just enough for a crisp lake breeze carrying the scent of fish, which was mingled with a strong summery aroma, to reach her nose. The scent spurred memories of the day Emma had met Patrick—a memory she'd woefully spent the last fifteen years trying to dispose of. Though twenty-eight years had passed after their first encounter, the memories were still as vivid as on that day, and he was still a major part of her life.

At forty-five, Emma knew Patrick McCarthy better than anyone. He was arrogant, charming, astonishingly good-looking, and a royal pain in her ass. If not for the fact that the two were still legally married, she couldn't have cared less about where he was, what he was doing, or who he was with.

Patrick had been Emma's first love, and in spite of everything that drove her away over the years, she was still smitten with him. From the moment they'd met at the homecoming dance in 1940, she was hooked. Patrick had a magnetism that made him different from other guys. Not only was he handsome, but he had a confidence and sense of adventure that enthralled her.

As a young woman, Emma had felt exuberant around him, like there wasn't anything in life she couldn't conquer. Once their relationship thrived, her dreams became his, and their hearts beat in sync, as their adolescent naiveté to the hardships of life catapulted them toward an uncertain future. Navigating a world at war, the two journeyed over the peaks and through the valleys of an unsettling period in American history, which had coincided with the beginning of their marriage.

Initially, the union achieved the desired amount of love and happiness Emma had expected from the confluence, but over time it left her vexed. As the pair struggled to find their way, work and friends eased the turmoil in their marriage, prolonging the urgency to acknowledge growing problems within it. Emma thought a child would change Patrick for the better, but it didn't. Eventually, the distinction of existing as Mrs. McCarthy morphed into drudgery, as he drove her to the edge of reason and fueled the constant conflict within over whether or not she wanted to continue in that capacity.

After they separated, Emma had moved to a quiet home on the shores of Eagle Lake in Southern Minnesota.

When he wasn't in DC, working on his cousin Eugene's congressional staff and presidential campaign, Patrick took up residence in a posh home on the cliffs overlooking St. Paul. Even without wondering, Emma always seemed to know where he was, since until recently, his antics were usually the center of attention whenever the family name was mentioned in the news.

Emma was shaken out of her thoughts by the bold smokey aroma of Columbian coffee that wafted toward the bedroom as it percolated in the kitchen. A true connoisseur of the beverage, she always made sure to set the automatic timer the night before so that the coffee would be ready as soon as she woke up. Shuffling wearily out of her bedroom and down the hall, making her way toward the kitchen, an untied fluffy, pink knee-length robe loosely draped her naked body, covering her sizable chest but exposing the rest of her buxom super model landscape. Stepping into the kitchen, she stretched and yawned, then took a deep breath of air, inhaling the delicious nutty smell coming from the coffee pot.

Pulling the robe together and tying it at the waist, she rubbed her eyes and groggily wandered over the brightly colored ceramic tiles, which sported a unique 1960s floral design, before stopping in front of the mahogany cabinets. While searching for her favorite coffee mug, more thoughts of her estranged husband entered Emma's head.

Outside, birds crooned to the dawn of a new day, and the rhythmic hum of an outboard motor propelled a small boat close to the shoreline. The sound of the engine and water churning caught her attention, drawing her to the kitchen window. Reporters often invaded her privacy as they circled out in the lake, like vultures hovering over roadkill. This was especially true when they wanted a picture, reaction, or comment regarding one of Patrick's reckless actions he'd committed the day before. But this morning, the noise seemed closer and more intense than usual. The boats weren't just trolling in the distance; they were static, and their motors idled closer to the shoreline than they ever had.

Peering around the cabinet door and through a bank of handcrafted casement windows, Emma looked at the reflection of the sun shimmering off the water and surrounding one of the boats like a halo. Streams of light struck the lake and landscape, reflecting the season's green palette, while a soft breeze plucked the leaves from the maple trees, as well as the winged seeds from the branches of the sycamores.

A piercing burst of light made Emma wince. Her eyes stung, and she soon became nauseous as an acidic solution entered her esophagus. As the room began to spin, every sound became thunderous. Her mind raced and her heart pounded. Blinded, she closed her eyes momentarily only to encounter an aura of intense shimmering spots and stars drifting through her darkened field of vision. Opening her eyes, she made an effort to rid her sight of the geometric shapes that were distorting her eyesight by carefully extracting her mug from its meticulous placement in the cupboard and closing the cabinet door. Emma suddenly had a premonition and could feel deep down in her core that something was very amiss.

Chimes from an exquisite grandfather clock, passed down from Emma's grandparents and located on the opposite end of the hall from the kitchen's entrance, rang in the ninth hour of the day, prompting Emma to examine an old electric clock that rested on a nearby counter. Carefully removing the pot of freshly brewed coffee from its warmer, she poured the scalding hot liquid into her cup, completely concentrating on the action to avoid the feelings that had consumed her only moments earlier. Lifting the mug to her lips, she took a sip of the nutty mixture as it flowed through her stomach and warmed it. The coffee pacified the heart-pounding wooziness she'd felt just moments ago, which she now attributed to caffeine withdrawal. Though the troubling occurrence had dissipated, an eerie ambiance interrupted the contentment she currently felt, as if something or someone had entered the house. In the past when Patrick came to visit their daughter Carrie, he had made it a habit to let himself in and sit at the table, working until she woke and he could spend a few hours with her.

Nervous and apprehensive, Emma left the kitchen and started walking down the hall, passing a credenza on the left, which was just outside the kitchen's entrance, and held a phone, small directory, and writing materials. The hall ultimately led to the home's front door, but one had to pass Tudor-arched door openings on the left and right to get there. When walking from the kitchen, the first door on the left opened to the dining room and the second to an expansive living room. Both featured large picture windows and French doors that led to a deck. Wrapping the home's exterior, the deck provided a serene view of Eagle Lake. As one walked from the kitchen, a staircase leading down to the basement sat just before the first door on the right side of the hall, opening to a half bath, while the second opened to the master suite.

Emma felt fearful. Her hand shook, causing the hot

liquid in her cup to drip onto her fingers. As she arrived at the room's entrance, she quietly cussed at the painful sensation she'd received from the burn. Maneuvering slowly around the corner, she expected to encounter him sitting at the table. Apprehensively she looked into the room, then sighed heavily, releasing a deep breath after finding the chairs vacant.

Over the years, the sizable oak table possessed an air of sleek English aristocratic style and had hosted dinners for some of the finest political figures in American history. It also bore witness to some of the best, and worst, moments in the couple's lives. But now it was relegated to little more than an extravagant fixture from their past, bridging eight decorative chairs that were infrequently occupied and only served as a conversation piece when friends came to call.

Pleased to discover everything was as it should be, Emma turned back toward the kitchen and collected herself. A cleansing breath escaped from her lungs when the phone resting on the credenza sprang to life. Alarmed, she dropped the cup, causing it to hit the ceramic floor with a violent impact as it shattered into tiny fragments.

Emma shrieked, then muffled the scream by placing both hands over her mouth. She carefully advanced toward the phone, her bare feet attempting to dodge the cup's broken pieces. The phone's bell reverberated once more throughout the house. When she arrived at the desk, habit forced her to glance at a small clock near the phone. Five minutes had passed since the Westminster chime of the grandfather clock had announced the top of the hour. Annoyed by the timing, she angrily removed the handset from its base.

"Hello!" she bellowed, anticipating the voice of a salesman on the other end, attempting to solicit one product or another. Instead, the sound of sobbing greeted her.

"Hello!" Emma grumbled with a heavy sigh.

"Mom?"

Emma could hear soft weeping and a crackling speaker echoing loudly in the background.

"Mom, it's Carrie."

It had been some time since they last spoke, but the voice of her twenty-three-year-old daughter had never sounded so tormented.

Carrie resided in Washington DC and had spent the last year working beside her father. She'd received a paid internship with Eugene McCarthy's campaign and had departed for the nation's capital shortly after graduating from the University of Minnesota with a degree in political science. In breaking the news to Emma about the move, Carrie informed her mother that it was the only way she could "learn the family business."

Initially, she was given work as a staff assistant and then moved on to rallying young adults to McCarthy's cause, rarely calling home or returning to Minnesota. When Carrie did come back, she preferred the urban rush of Dinkytown, located near the University of Minnesota campus, to the rural serenity of Eagle Lake.

"Carrie, I'm having a hard time hearing you," Emma barked as she adjusted the phone's volume. The breeze outside had intensified, causing the tree's branches to thump loudly against the windows, which only increased Emma's frustration as she struggled to hear what her daughter was saying.

The unpleasant feeling Emma had encountered earlier in the kitchen had returned. Carrie's long hesitation in speaking was most certainly the sign of menacing news, which immediately sent shivers down her spine. It was difficult to understand Carrie's distorted voice, which was being suffocated by continuous announcements from a loudspeaker in the background.

"Carrie, are you alright?" She cupped her hand over her other ear to block the sounds coming from outside.

"Mom!" Another long pause followed. "Mom... it's Dad!" Carrie's tone was somber.

For a second, Emma relaxed and thanked God that Carrie was all right. For as gratifying as it was to feel a release of tension from the base of her neck and shoulders, there was still an unpleasant feeling churning in her stomach, which only intensified when she remembered that Carrie had said, "It's Dad." It wasn't the first time Emma had this feeling. Years earlier, her stomach had soured on the day she learned that Patrick was as mortal as everyone else. It was also the day he'd changed in ways she never imagined he could.

"What's the problem? What's wrong with him?" she grunted, assuming it was one of his crazy capers to blame again. It had been years since she had seen him in person, though stories of his life and endeavors had been splashed prominently in the news they were now mired behind those of his senator cousin running for president.

The wind outside continued its attack, as Carrie's garbled words mellowed, leaving an awkward silence in their wake.

Emma paced back and forth. The silence on the other end of the line was now intermittently interrupted by

Carrie's occasional sniffles and attempts to speak. The hall felt cold, and the tile floor chilled the soles of her bare feet. Emma cradled the handset between her ear and shoulder as she tightened the sash on her robe and crossed her arms over her chest.

The static from the long-distance call crackled in her ear, leading her to believe she may have lost the connection, but another deep breath and sniffle alerted her to Carrie's presence.

"He's been shot! He's still alive, but I have a bad feeling that he's not going to make it!" Carrie cried out, struggling to pronounce the words as her voice trembled violently.

"Shot?" Emma questioned, stopping in the entryway to the dining room. "How?" she exclaimed.

"Haven't you been listening to the news?"

"No, Carrie, I haven't."

The temperature in both the hallway and the dining room seemed to drop even lower with the announcement. A passing cloud outside obstructed the light, and the house seemed to groan with each gust of wind.

"Why would anyone, other than me, want to shoot that bastard?" She thought honestly to herself. He was arrogant, possessed a big ego, and excessively abused alcohol. To those unacquainted with his true nature, he was regarded as an admirable person. Like his cousin Gene, God had blessed him with wit, charm, and an astonishing ability to appeal to the average person.

The wind finally died down, and the house's foundation creaked, while the old clock at the end of the hall announced the bottom of the hour passing.

"He's not going to make it; I'm sure of it!" Carrie's tone sounded bleaker and more definitive.

11

"Where are you?" Emma inquired.

In a tired voice, Carrie replied, "Atlanta. We flew to Birmingham, Alabama, for a quick campaign stop and then flew on to Atlanta."

Hearing the mention of Alabama infuriated Emma. She had spent a good portion of what she referred to as "a shitty year" in Alabama with Patrick, and she despised the south. The word alone made her hot and sweaty as memories of the past raced through her head. She shook as visions of the day in which she metaphorically lost Patrick flooded her mind and played over and over again, like an old black-and-white movie. Losing him psychologically long ago in that portion of the country had been grievous; losing him physically there now would only be callous.

"Cousin Gene flew down to make a stop in Birmingham, and then we went on to Atlanta to meet with a group of African Americans from the Fulton County Democratic Party. He received word that the party chairman had handpicked an all-white delegation to the Democratic National Convention, most of whom had openly pledged their support for George Wallace. Gene wanted to stir the pot a little, so he thought he would meet with black representatives from the party. We arrived around 3:00 p.m. and drove to the motel, where we met with a number of black leaders about a rival delegation to the DNC," Carrie continued, sounding clearly exhausted while she attempted to bring her mother up to speed.

"After the meeting, we were supposed to depart on a tour of an area known as Vine City, then go to dinner..." Her voice faltered as she described the scene. "So, around 5:00 p.m., we finished the meeting and were departing the motel entrance, when it sounded like someone set off a bunch of firecrackers just outside the door".

Emma's heart sank, and a knot formed in her throat. She knew where this was going. Emma tightened her hold on the receiver and pressed it firmly against her ear, leaning back against the opening that formed the arched doorway that led into the dining room. Slowly she lowered herself and sat on the floor.

"Stop... stop... stop!" she uttered, unconsciously bringing her knees to her robed chest. "I can't do this!" crept out of her mouth as she wrapped one arm around her well-toned legs. Her robe had ridden up when she had slid to the floor, exposing her body from the waist down. Sitting on the chilly tiles, she lowered her forehead, allowing it to rest on her knees as she sighed heavily.

"Mom, you have to come down here," Carrie petitioned. "Legally, you're still his wife, and I can't make decisions for him."

Emma could hear a loudspeaker in the background, paging hospital personnel.

For years, Emma and Carrie had been at odds over Patrick. To Emma, Carrie was Daddy's little girl and far too loyal to the man who had left her behind after years of standing by his side and caring for him. Carrie's lack of trips to Eagle Lake and the scarcity of contact between them had only added to the tension and further angered Emma.

In Carrie's opinion, there was no time or place for her to give credence to her mother's bitter rhetoric, as it pertained to her father. What was done was done, and it was time to get over it and move on. Each time Carrie had visited, she grew more and more jaded over her mother's constant needling about her father's affairs and her negativity toward him. Eventually, she preferred to seek refuge among friends, rather than listen to endless rants about "that man," as her mother scornfully referred to him.

"I can't, Carrie. I just can't," Emma retorted with a heavy sigh, her face hidden behind her long hair, which was beautifully blended with the blonde of her youth and the silver of her longevity. "I have been in this type of situation before with that man, and I won't go through it again! You will have to handle it."

"Mom, I'm not *asking* you! You need to suck it up and get down here!" Carrie sounded clearly annoyed. "I don't understand why you hate him so much? You never divorced him and it's no secret that you still love him!" Her voice softened, exposing what they both knew to be true.

"Carrie, he hurt me too many times!" A pained expression crossed her face. The heavy footfall of wooden heels clunking the hospital's tile floor suppressed the phone lines crackle as men in oxfords shuffled sluggishly toward her daughter.

"There will be an airline ticket waiting for you at Minneapolis-St. Paul International," Carrie snapped as the noise in the hospital's corridor grew more intense. Emma could hear reporters asking Carrie for comment on her dad.

"I'm going to have to go, but before I do—" She was interrupted by a volley of questions that were being hurled at her from the reporters. Talking over the reporters, Carrie continued, "North Central Airlines, flight 450 leaving at 7:20 p.m. for Chicago O'Hare. Are you writing this down? You need to write this down."

"Hold on," Emma said as she reached for the pad and pen she kept by the phone. She quickly scribbled what Carrie had just told her. "Okay. Got it. Go ahead."

"You will land there around 9:20 p.m. and connect to Delta Airlines, flight number 121 to Atlanta at 3:10 a.m., their time, and arrive around 5:45 a.m.!" Carrie shouted into the phone, ignoring the reporters' questions.

"We are at Georgia Baptist Hospital, Room 114," was the last sentence Emma heard before the connection was lost.

"Carrie? Hello? Wait!" Emma yelled, lifting her head to check the cord and its connection to the handset. Nothing but the constant drone of a dial tone could be heard. She released the receiver, letting it drop to the floor.

"Shit!" she shouted, cradling her head in her hands. Often, she had contemplated receiving a call similar to this one, with the assumption their marriage would have ended by this point, and legally, she would not be obligated to spousal responsibilities. Time and time again, she wanted to petition for divorce, but one thing or another always took precedence over her need to complete the action.

Deep down, Emma never truly gave up hope that one day Patrick would leave the craziness behind and return to what they had in their youth. Her eyes welled up, raining tears down onto her exposed legs and feet. "Damn it!" she thought angrily to herself, pushing her long blonde locks away from her face.

The steady dial tone coming through the receiver gave way to an obnoxious pulse drawing her attention. Tilting her head to peer at the handset, Emma began to sob uncontrollably as she thought about the past. There were too many experiences, both positive and negative, for it to end this way. Patrick had survived other traumatic events even when he wasn't expected to, so maybe, she wagered, he would beat the odds once more. The fact that she felt this way again was maddening, but the rhythm of her heart fluttering anxiously in time with the grandfather clock's pendulum became more noticeable, as the pulse from the phone gave way to silence.

Blinking back tears, Emma placed her hand into one of the robe's oversized pockets in search of a tissue to catch the deluge flowing from her eyes. An unexpected sensation greeted her touch drawing attention to a silky smooth garment sliding up the side of her bare leg as she brought it toward her face. Gulping down a sob, she attempted to focus on the ornate blue and white garment now draped over her fingers and dangling between her knees. A cherished accessory, the scarf had been given to her by Patrick on the day of their wedding. Having worn it the day before, she recalled hastily retrieving it from the bed and placing it in her pocket before pulling back the covers and removing her robe. Often fashionably worn around her neck, the multicolored strands of silk held positive memories of a simpler time. A time her soul yearned and body ached for. Blurry-eyed, she slid the material between her fingertips as an audible sniffle of hope drew into her lungs.

"He's alive!" she muttered incoherently staring at the scarf while tears continued to swirl down her cheeks. Emma couldn't help feeling disdain that she may still actually give a damn about him.

"I can feel it...he's alive."

16

FAMILY TIES

Chapter Two

July 19, 1968—State Route 60

"Why didn't I listen to my father?" She asked herself guiding her Pontiac Bonneville over the rough country road leading her toward Minneapolis. Anytime one of Patrick's shenanigans thrust her or the family into the spotlight she repeated the same question to herself. "He always said Patrick and I were cut from a different cloth." She checked her looks in the rearview mirror. "I see that now. I don't even recognize the well-mannered person my dad raised me to be." She thought to herself. "Hell, even my personality has changed." Her eyes returned to the road ahead of her as she thought about her parents.

Born to an affluent family, Emma Dickinson desired little as a child, since most things were given to her without having to ask for them. Her father, Edward—a prominent physician of English ancestry—ensured her every need was taken care of. Tall, handsome, strong-willed, and intelligent, Edward was well-liked by most he came into contact with.

The son of a surgeon, medicine surrounded his world at an early age and continued as a constant throughout his college years at the University of Minnesota. After graduation in 1917, there was little doubt as to where the down-to-earth intern would take up residency, since his father held the title of Head Surgeon at St. Joseph's Hospital in St. Paul. His unassuming and confident demeanor quickly won over other doctors and staff, who were envious of his connection and doubtful of his abilities. Furthermore, they were jealous of his Rudolph Valentino good looks. Hard work and long hours brought new challenges and great personal reward—but left little time for social interaction outside of the hospital—so it was only natural that he met nurse Emily Bowes, the daughter to one of his father's colleagues, at St. Joseph's.

Emma recalled the pictures she'd seen of her mother, a beautiful woman of Anglo-Saxon heritage. In them she could see her mother Emily's conservative demeanor, radiant smile—and through the black-and-white photography—the dishwater blonde hair that had caught her father's attention. She remembered how her father always spoke of her mother's light, fruity, and floral fragrance that pleasantly lingered while she was near, captivating his senses and aiding in her angelic appearance.

Emma's mother, Emily, whom she was named after, had immigrated to the United States with her parents—Dr. Henry and Anne Bowes—after fearing the German advance through Belgium could lead to their doorstep in Eastbourne, England. The family departed Liverpool on June 28, 1914, after Emma's grandparents had determined that leaving the island for the United States was the most sensible thing to do.

Leaving Eastbourne in fear was the last thing Emily thought her parents would consider, and she had vehemently opposed the idea when it was presented.

Grandfather Bowes had told Emma of the loss he'd seen reflected in her mother's eyes as they watched the English coastline disappear into the distance. He often spoke of the family's frigid and blustery journey across the North Atlantic. The stories he provided her with painted a harsh vision of the crossing as the descriptive words he used told of strong winds extracting arctic air from the ocean's surface, whipping it over the ship's steel rails, across the deck, and into the ship's interior spaces.

Through his stories, Emma envisioned the inside of the ship's cabin. At times it was as though she could almost smell the sea salt and feel the damp, icy feeling that chilled her mother to the bone. Grandpa Bowes recounted how her mother would seek shelter from the cold on her bunk wrapped in the bulky, white medallion quilt Emma now possessed, which her grandmother—known only to her as Nanna—had passed down to her mother only days before Nanna's death.

Nanna's quilt was a magnificent achievement. The central motif of the captivating work emphasized a large eight-point diamond blue star at its center. Four of the star's rays extended from the center toward each edge—as though they were points on a compass—while the other four rays, which were shorter in length, designated points in between the compass headings and radiated out toward each corner. From turquoise to royal, various shades of blue, sprayed out from the center until the deep blue intersected with patches of white as it bordered the dark and trimmed the star, then diffused to gray and black before repeating the original pattern to the quilt's edge.

Her grandmother's quilt was Emma's most prized possession, and when not displayed on top of an old trunk at the end of her bed, it lay elegantly on the foot of her bed as a memorial to her mother and grandmother. Emma often wrapped herself in the patchwork, conceptualizing how her mother felt wrapped in its warmth, frightened of what awaited her in the United States.

If the voyage alone wasn't enough to unnerve her mother, Emma gained a sense through the stories she'd listened to that Emily had unraveled shortly after arriving in New York City, when her father had announced his decision to forward the family to St. Paul, Minnesota. Grandpa Bowes' decision to leave his well-established family, who'd already emigrated to the United States, infuriated her mother.

Emma's grandmother laughed when she told her stories as to how her mother thought of St. Paul as "frontier-like," and filled with "cowboys and Indians." But she quickly learned it wasn't. She had also told her, "Your mother grew to love Minnesota. She adored the bright twinkling stars, which flickered reassuringly in the sky behind Polaris. She would sit for hours and stare into the sky, reaching out for the heavens as if the stars were close enough to touch in the darkness of night. The sparkling North Star comforted her and was like a sign from the heavens, letting us know that Nanna was watching over us, and she was meant to be there."

Emma cherished the stories her grandparents had told her about her mother, and how her parents had fallen in love. Emma's father refused to open up about the events from the day she was born, so all that she knew about the fate of the woman who had given her life came from the stories her grandparents conveyed to her.

It was clear to Emma that her parents had complemented one another, and it was no surprise that her father, a physician, and mother, a nurse, had fallen in love while working together at St. Joseph's Hospital in St. Paul.

Driving along, Emma thought about how she had often prayed for that type of love—the type which Grandpa Bowes referred to as eternal. He would tell her that's why her father never spoke of her mother's death. "He refused to accept the love they'd shared was gone just because your mother wasn't physically on earth," he'd tell her. "Just because her body was gone didn't mean her spirit was."

Her grandfather always bowed his head and stared at the floor when he spoke of her mother. Tears would flow from the ducts of his large round eyes, over his firm cheekbones, and into a thick, gray beard, which dated his wrinkled face. "I remember how your father sprinted from the hospital to assist your mother with the delivery. They were so excited." Grandpa always added that tidbit as though it were happening all over again. "Your dad told me how after you arrived he'd lifted you to your mother's bosom as they wept and laughed, cuddling you. Nothing seemed wrong until your mother suddenly lost consciousness. Soon after he noticed a pool of fluid collecting on the floor beside the bed. He watched in horror as blood dripped steadily from the corner of your great-grandmother's quilt covering the lower half of your mother. He did what he could to stop the hemorrhage, but he was helpless to save her."

Emma played the second part of his narration through

her head. "He would always look up at me and smile through his tears. He'd tell me how lucky I was to have such loving parents, and how fortunate they were to have me."

Watching the countryside roll by, she thought to herself, "I wonder what my mother would say now?"

Emma's mind raced as she sped down State Route 60 toward Faribault. Ahead, the small farm town of Elysian approaching made her lift her foot from the gas pedal, allowing the car to slow and ceding time for her to collect her thoughts as she eased into the ribbed, white leather bench seat supporting her burden. Exhaling loudly her forearm slumped over the armrest dividing the driver's seat from the passenger's. Suddenly, silence surrounded her, offset only by the purr coming from the Bonneville's 265 horsepower engine and the hum of its vulcanized tires rolling over the bituminous surface below.

Two hours had gone by since Carrie's phone call. In that time, Emma had bathed, dressed, packed a bag, and put thirteen miles behind her. She had performed these actions in an almost zombie-like state.

"God, I need a cigarette!" she uttered, mulling over the morning's events. "Shit!" she cursed aloud while half-heartedly searching the vehicle for a pack. Her father condemned her smoking habit and had blamed Patrick for introducing it to her.

"If he only knew the truth!" She cleverly grinned as she observed the rows of corn lining both sides of the two-lane road. "Hmmm, there used to be a Texaco station along this route. I believe they sell cigarettes there too," she muttered to herself while searching for the station.

Over the years, Emma had become a "sneaky smoker,"

as she liked to call it. Since her father detested the habit, she resorted to sneaking cigarettes whenever family and friends were around and then attempting to cover the foul smell by using a sweet perfume. The habit had begun in college. Initially, it was a social mechanism medical students utilized in order to pass the time between studies. Then after Patrick's accident, it had become a way to alleviate hours of stress and boredom.

Her father had suspected she was smoking, so when he uncovered her secret, he was furious. "You are a medical professional!" He scolded her like a little child. "You know better!"

"Yes, Daddy, I know better!" she quipped aloud to herself, guiding the Bonneville over the oncoming lane and into the service station. Approaching an island holding two fuel pumps, she slowed to a stop and noticed a young man sauntering toward her from the station's office. Wrestling the weighty driver's side door open, Emma stepped from the vehicle and gathered herself.

Standing in a stupor, the attendant stared at her curvaceous figure. Tastefully clothed in a powder-blue fit-and-flare dress with a Kensington stand collar, Emma's style screamed Jackie Kennedy, but the body within howled Marilyn Monroe. The garment's V-neck smartly accentuated her sizable bosom, while its snug tailored cut emphasized the curvature of her derriere. Three-quarter length sleeves crowned by expansive two-inch cuffs highlighted her rosy-white skin. A stitched waistline was the only obvious boundary separating the top of the dress from the pleated bottom. Enhancing her thin midriff, the dress's waistline gradually flowed out to her knees. Her shapely calves, free of any stockings, were on full display.

And a pair of high heels that were color-coordinated to match her dress completed the outfit.

"Fill up the gas, check the oil, and wash the windows," Emma instructed smugly. "Oh ... and close your mouth!" she added.

"Check the oil and wash the windows?" the attendant questioned her.

"Yes! Do you have a problem with that?" She smirked, throwing a small purse over her arm and closing the car door.

"No, ma'am," the young man answered hesitantly as Emma made her way toward the small shop attached to a vehicle repair bay.

"Damn kids!" she whispered under her breath. "I'm not old enough to be called ma'am yet! And whatever happened to the good old days of full service?" Emma wondered, frustrated by what she perceived as the lack of respect that kids showed their elders in the modern world.

Arriving at the service desk, she removed the bag from her arm, placed it on the counter, and proceeded to wait for the attendant to return to his post. Ten minutes had passed before the teenager made his way into the small office. Reeking of petroleum, he was forced to pass within inches of Emma as he moved to position himself behind the counter. Wiping his hands with a dirty rag stained with gas and grease, he began clicking the old cash register's soiled levers to complete the sale.

"Did you get any in the tank?" Emma joked sarcastically after noticing one of his khaki-colored pant legs was saturated with gas.

"Yes, ma'am," the attendant responded, embarrassed, as he shook his leg and fanned the immense stain. "I checked the oil and washed your window as well. "That'll be $6.80," he added.

"$6.80? It's gas, not gold!" Emma thundered.

"Well, ma'am, nowadays gas is gold." He chuckled.

Reluctantly, Emma removed her pocketbook from her purse and withdrew $7.00, setting the cash on the wooden countertop.

"Add in a pack of Old Gold Filters to that," Emma ordered, as the sound of hammering echoed throughout the building, drawing her to the attached vehicle bay.

Reaching to a shelf behind him, the attendant retrieved a pack of cigarettes and placed them on the counter. "That'll be $7.30." He smiled jovially.

As she lowered her head and gaze toward her purse to take out the rest of the money, a strand of hair dangled menacingly over her nose. Crossing her eyes to view the tress, Emma released a strong puff of air from her lungs and defiantly blew the blondish gray strand from her face. A satisfied grin crossed her profile, as her gaze returned to her pocketbook to rummage around for change.

"Just take it out of this." She added a dollar to the counter.

"Out of eight dollars, seventy cents is your change." He placed the change and the pack of cigarettes in her open hand.

"Thanks," she commented smartly, dropping the items into her purse, then securing the top before slinging the bag over her arm.

"Have a nice day!" the attendant added as Emma turned to make her way out of the station and back to the Bonneville.

Tossing her purse through the open driver's side

window and into the passenger seat, she muscled open the car's door, got in, yanked it closed, and made herself comfortable. Checking her hair in the rearview mirror, she was troubled by her appearance.

"I'm too damn young to be this gray!" She pensively mused as she ensured each strand made it back into place. "God, I used to have great hair." She enlarged her pupils and flared her nostrils. The image in the mirror reflected a physical version vastly different from the one she'd imagined.

"I don't feel like shit, so why do I look like shit?" Emma pondered, poking at the puffiness under her eyes. She recalled how Patrick had loved staring into her big blue eyes while he stroked her long, silky blonde hair. He would run his fingers through it as they lounged in the grass at Diamond Point Park, watching small pleasure boats churn the water and traverse Lake Bemidji. In the distance, the hollowness of logs contacting the ground could be heard as trucks unloaded their cargo at the sawmills on the far side of the lake. Even now, Emma could recall the woodsy spice emitting from a variety of native Minnesotan trees as they were being cut and processed. Similar to the scent of cedar stored in an old hope chest, the aroma permeated Bemidji's air, adding to its frontier feel and Lumberjack toughness.

A swift shake of her head and a cleansing breath tucked the memory back into its rightful region of her brain, like a library book set back in its place on the shelf. Donning a square pair of color-coordinated Monaco sunglasses, Emma retracted the power top, and shifted the Bonneville into drive, pulling away from the station.

Emma returned her thoughts to the current situation

as she accelerated on the gas pedal and made her way out of town. With her left hand on the wheel, she utilized her right to snatch her purse from the passenger seat. After pulling it into her lap and popping it open, she quickly removed the soft white pack of cigarettes from inside. Flipping the pack upside down, she pounded the top against her left wrist, compressing the tobacco in each stick toward the filter.

"The cigarette for independent people. Well, I'm as independent as it gets," she snickered as she placed one between her lips. Reaching toward the lower portion of the dash, she pulled the ashtray toward her and engaged a silver cigarette lighter within the compartment, triggering its heating element. Within seconds, the lighter sprung back, indicating it was ready for use. Emma removed the lighter and lit her cigarette.

"Ah, that's it!" She inhaled deeply, feeling the nicotine create the euphoria that fulfilled her addiction. Satisfied, she returned the lighter to its holder and settled back into her seat.

"Not so sure I'd agree it's the richest tobacco flavor I have ever tasted but it works." She exhaled deeply.

Now eager for information, Emma enlisted the help of the vehicle's AM radio. With a click and a twist of the selector knob, Minnesota's news and information station crackled over the speakers. Less than thirty minutes into the two-hour journey to the airport, the hum of the vehicle's engine whirred behind a light piano jazz piece, only to be interrupted by a stoic voice cutting into the music.

"We interrupt this program with this bulletin just in from our WCCO news bureau in Atlanta, Georgia. It's believed Minnesota Senator Eugene McCarthy and an aide were shot as they left the motel where a meeting they had attended had just concluded. We repeat, news coming from Atlanta indicates Minnesota Senator Eugene McCarthy and an unidentified aide were shot late yesterday afternoon while leaving a motel in Atlanta. We are waiting on updates from our partner news organization in Atlanta. As we receive more details, we promise to pass them along to you. We now continue with our scheduled programming."

"My God," Emma thought aloud to herself after the radio confirmed the information her daughter had provided. Her eyes welled with tears, blurring her sight and hindering her ability to follow the road ahead. Stepping on the brake pedal, the Bonneville slowed, then rolled to a stop on the shoulder of the road. "King, Kennedy, and now two McCarthys. What in the hell is this world coming to?" She sniffled, wiping her eyes carefully with the back of her right hand and taking great care not to burn herself with the red hot end of the cigarette.

"What drives men to commit such a heinous act?" she wondered, taking an extended drag from her cigarette.

Over the years, Emma had taught herself to ignore the political rhetoric spewing from both sides of the legislative aisle, though she remained abreast of the issues affecting the nation—especially issues relevant to the McCarthy family, since Eugene had announced his intent to challenge Lyndon Johnson for the Democratic Party's nomination and presidency last November. She was extremely cognizant of how popular Eugene's stance against the war in Vietnam had become with the nation's youth, and how politically dangerous it was to openly stand against a member of his own political party, who just so happened to be the sitting president of the United States. After mulling over the information that Carrie had rapidly relayed over the phone, she determined the reason for the assassination attempt was definitely more significant than war or politics, and since it had occurred in the South, it was painfully obvious it involved Eugene's stance on civil rights.

To the white supremacists, Eugene or anyone else with the courage to stand before them on their own turf and challenge their ideology was a serious threat to their existence. In their opinion, Eugene was a turncoat and deserved to meet the same fate as others who had confronted them. After listening to the radio announcement, it appeared clear to Emma the racists had gotten what they wanted.

HER FATHER'S DAUGHTER

Chapter Three

------◆------

July 19, 1968—Driving toward Faribault

Releasing the brake and actuating the gas pedal, Emma's heart pounded as she left the shoulder of the road and continued on. Boldly she flicked her cigarette into the wind, sparking a determination of old and a doggedness born out of necessity and generated from within by Edward. She thought about her father and how he had managed to recover after her mother's death. Driving on, she continued to recall stories her grandparents had acquainted her with regarding his mental constitution and lengthy recovery.

Following her mother's death and funeral, Edward immersed himself in his medical duties and Emma's care. Edward's parents had decorated the room where Emily had perished with memories of their son and daughter-in-law's love and life together. The quilt which covered her as she crossed to the afterlife had been carefully washed and dried by Edward's mother. She'd placed the patchwork in the same cedar chest containing Emily's wedding dress and had stowed it in the attic, since Edward couldn't bear to look at the quilt, but refused to dispose of it.

When not at work, Edward spent hours in Emily's room, traversing the floor with baby Emma in his arms and talking to his wife as if she were still there. The practice troubled many in Edward's and Emily's families, who feared a slip from reality, but as time passed, the convention proved more therapeutic than manic, assisting him through the loss as he learned how to cope with Emily's death.

As Emma advanced in age, her mother's room and its contents seemed to possess an energy that fascinated and delighted her. Often she would encounter her father there, quietly perusing medical papers detailing the latest medical gadgets and findings, as he rocked methodically in a vintage wooden chair made of oak. The room and the papers produced questions, which stimulated conversation between the two, leading to stories about Emma's mother that would last for hours. While immersed in the warm odors of pine and cedar, which brought a woodland fragrance to the room, Emma loved listening to her father's version of her parents' introduction and romance. Through her father's stories, she learned about the mutual love she and her mother had for silviculture, thus the reason for her adoration of woodsy smells.

On occasion, she would visit her mother's room to engage her spirit in conversation. Often Emma would find this item or that, precariously placed in a different location. She assumed her father had moved the articles, until one day when she realized Edward hadn't been home to relocate the items.

Edward had contemplated moving from the home on numerous occasions after Emily's death, but he always concluded it was just too difficult to leave the dwelling. He resolved that the familiarity of the home and the memories contained within made it easier for him to manage the challenges of fatherhood alone. The decision proved to be wise, since family resided nearby and assisted in Emma's care while Edward worked long hours at the hospital.

As the years slipped by, Emma flourished into a strong and self-sufficient young lady. Though her grandparents regularly checked in on her after school during the week and during the day on weekends, she primarily cared for herself, assuming most of the domestic responsibilities at a much earlier age than other kids, despite Edward's insistence she concentrate solely on her studies. Emma had been gifted with an intelligence that allowed her to excel in school, thus her grades were never an issue. Superior marks kept the good doctor off her back and gave her space to pursue whatever she desired after class.

By the age of fourteen, she often found herself alone in the early hours of the evening, as she required less supervision and assistance from her grandparents. For companionship, friends from school and the neighborhood often stopped by to socialize. When they didn't come over, she would pass the time by singing to light music as it crackled over a compact Atwater Kent cathedral radio. Never despairing in her predicament, she often thought about her mother and what she might've been like in her youth as she went about her day with a smile. Grandfather Bowes had assured Emma that she was an exact replica of her mother. Her beautiful appearance and captivating singing warmed the home in the winter, and on hot summer days, her voice carried out into the street, bringing comfort to passersby.

By the time she turned sixteen, Emma's silver screen beauty merged with an astute sense of self, which made her a success at her father's social engagements. A happy young lady of refined grace and balance, she often accompanied Edward at hospital functions to the disappointment of women vying for his attention. Buoyant in any situation, Emma's controlled disposition was often misinterpreted as conceit, until she engaged in conversation, which demonstrated her true character. Some envied the sparkle in her smile and the adoration she received when entering a room, while others found pleasure in the glow her congenial allure brought to the dull events.

Fearless of stature or age, Emma stood diminutive beside her father as she engaged in conversation and confounded those who assumed she was nothing more than a child. Emma delighted in watching her father socialize with politicians, attorneys, and other physicians, marveling as men of prominence listened intently to his counsel. Privately she pondered the reason her father had remained working at the hospital for as long as he had when it was apparent he was destined to achieve more. Initially, she deduced he stayed out of deference to her mother's memory. From one perspective, it seemed only natural that her father would cling to the corridors where their romance had commenced. But after re-examining her theory, she also determined that the lengthy tenure had as much to do with profession and tradition as it did with memory-laden passages.

A year had passed since Emma's grandfather retired

from his hospital administrator position at St. Joseph's. For fourteen years, his vision and leadership had driven the organization to prominence and changed the way hospitals around the region provided care to their patients. Aspiring to walk in his father's footsteps, Edward optimistically waited for the hospital's board of trustees to present him with the opportunity to extend his father's vision. When the board decided to accept resumes in lieu of appointing a director from within, Edward began to search for an administrator position elsewhere. After twenty-three years of dedicated service, thirteen of which he served as head surgeon, Edward tendered his resignation, no longer content to wait in the wings for a role he was more than qualified to perform—even if it meant he would have to go elsewhere.

The day Edward removed his personal items from the hospital was bittersweet. Although thrilled by the promising opportunity that Lutheran Hospital in Bemidji, Minnesota, offered, he found it difficult to clean twenty-three years' of memories from the desk he'd occupied and leave the place where he'd met Emily. Emma was supportive, standing just inside the door to his office as acquaintances and colleagues dropped by to bid him good luck and farewell, then departed hurriedly to their assignments. Doctors and nurses alike had verbalized their frustration regarding the board's decision to search for an outside candidate and had professed their respect and understanding regarding Edward's decision to leave, though the encouragement provided little relief from the fact that he hadn't even been considered. Any doubts he'd had previously about moving on came to an abrupt halt upon the discovery of an old white envelope that had his name written on the front and had been placed in his bottom desk drawer.

Lifting the envelope to the light, Edward had no memory of having seen this envelope before. But then he realized the writing was Emily's. Scrambling to open it, Edward trembled in disbelief as he lifted the pointed flap that secured the correspondence. Bewildered, he slowly lowered himself into an old, brown leather chair, which had borne the weight of his triumphs and tragedies over the years. Perched precariously on the edge of his seat, Edward pored over what was the last note Emily had written.

May 7, 1923
My darling Edward,

Your love and devotion have guided our family in the same way it will guide your surgical staff. You are the best man for the position; never doubt your capabilities or my support.

Your loving wife,
Emily

Eager to see what her father had found, Emma crossed the room to gaze over his shoulder. She recognized her mother's handwriting from the other items in the house that contained Emily's writing. Emma drew in close to read the letter. Even though years had passed since her death, Emily's strong emotions still could be deciphered by the dark ink etched on the paper. The slant of her calligraphy accentuated her enthusiasm, and the loop of each letter conveyed great pride in her husband's accomplishments. Spellbound, Emma stood enamored of

35

her mother's writing as the words rolled off the paper and into her heart, intensifying the bond already existing between them.

Sitting in the chair, Edward's eyes lifted slowly, as he stared off vacantly into the distance. The letter fell from his grasp and landed in his lap. He reflected on their time together, and thoughts of her delicate touch drew him in deeper as images of Emily came to life before him. Their souls communicated without words or interference. For the first time since her death, Edward had finally found solace in the desperate measures he had taken to save her so long ago.

Even though Emma could not physically see her mother's image, she could feel the adoration her mother felt for both of them through the warm radiant sensations her written words had released. Like gentle ocean swells, the script rolled over them, and they waded in what Emily's spirit emitted—a message of love, absolution, congratulations, and approval of Edward's decision.

With his doubts about taking the position and leaving the hospital and St. Paul behind now firmly gone, Edward felt comforted in knowing that Emily's spirit would reside within them, regardless of where he was. She would always be there watching over them. Now at peace, Edward knew Emily was as proud of him today as she had been the day she composed the note. Fortitude provided opportunities, and Emily's undying love made it purposeful.

SUMMER LOVE

Chapter Four

July 19, 1968–A&W

The older and bumpier bituminous surface of State Route 60, just west of Faribault, soon gave way to the newer and freshly paved Interstate 35, which ran north toward Minneapolis, signaling to Emma that she was getting closer to the halfway point of her destination. Just outside of town, the government had invested a substantial amount of money and time into constructing a new road to link Minneapolis to Faribault. For all that had been done to circumvent the city's business district, a portion remained in the final stages of completion, and stop lights still stood as an obstacle, interrupting traffic flow along the stretch that would soon become a highway.

"Your tax dollars at work!" she grumbled, entering a completed portion of the interstate momentarily before encountering stop lights swinging over the intersection and incomplete segment.

With a little over an hour of travel time left, the Bonneville's engine droned on. An intense sulfur scent rose from the road and filled Emma's nostrils with the stench of petroleum, reminding her of the awful smell radiating from the gas station attendant's trousers. A jazzy sound delivered through the speakers enhanced the transitory scenery as it continued to play discreetly under the hum of the car's engine. There hadn't been an update in some time regarding the situation in Atlanta, and Emma was growing impatient for information.

Notwithstanding the putrid smell of asphalt, the scenery, music, engine, and road noise lulled Emma's mind into a comfortable reflection of her past as she put a few more miles behind her. For years, she had asked herself when and where it was she went wrong in her relationship with Patrick. And each time, she went back to his accident.

"That's when it all changed; that's when he became someone else. But even from the beginning, something was off." Considered to be from a blue-collar business family, Patrick's parents were very astute, well-educated, and admired in the community. Patrick's mother and father had moved to Bemidji from Watkins, Minnesota, in the mid-1930s after his grandfather died. For a long time, Emma wondered if the problem with their marriage had been there from the start of their relationship, and maybe it wasn't the accident that initiated his behavior? Maybe it was the difference in their rearing, genealogy, or gentility, but each time she attempted to blame other elements. She recanted and cast blame on issues and events surrounding their lives.

Lost in contemplation, she was suddenly brought out of her thoughts by one of the radio station announcers interrupting the music. Emma increased the volume to hear the man better. "We interrupt programming for this important bulletin from our WCCO news bureau. It's believed Minnesota senator Eugene McCarthy and an aide were shot yesterday afternoon as they left a motel in Atlanta, Georgia. Details are slowly coming in from our correspondent who is now at Georgia Baptist Hospital where both men were taken. According to information obtained from one of the senator's staff members, a meeting had occurred at the motel between Senator McCarthy and members of Georgia's Democratic Party. The meeting had concluded, and the men were departing the motel when shots rang out. The informant confirmed that a senior aide, Patrick McCarthy, who is also the senator's cousin, was hit by at least one bullet, but the informant had no knowledge if the senator had been struck. Our reporter at Georgia Baptist Hospital is working hard to obtain information on both the senator and his aide's condition. We will pass along more information as soon as we receive it."

Familiar with the majority of the information presented, Emma gave little thought to the update while returning the volume to its previous level. Partially engaged in the act of listening and driving, she let her mind continue questioning the past.

Feeling tired and overwhelmed by the drive and events, Emma sought somewhere to pull over and rest for a bit. Her stomach had begun to churn as she passed through Faribault. It growled angrily, making it difficult to concentrate as it reminded Emma that breakfast had consisted solely of a cup of coffee and a cigarette. An A&W restaurant stood on the outskirts of town and close to the road. For as long as she could remember, the Allen and

Wright restaurant chain had been her favorite place to eat a pizza burger and get a frosty mug of root beer. It was the perfect spot to take a break, purchase some comfort food to calm her stomach, and relax in the comfort of her own car.

With ample time remaining to get to the airport, she directed the Bonneville off the road and turned it into the restaurant's parking lot, moving slowly until she came to a stop next to a large menu set atop a short post and covered in plexiglass. Adjacent to the menu, a large metal two-way speaker sat, which was silver in color and matching those often used at drive-in movies. Renowned for its car-side service, the outdoor attraction shaded its patrons and their vehicles under a metal canopy. The restaurant also featured servers, known as car hops, who brought the order to the car and attached the food tray to the vehicle's partially open window.

Placing her car in park, she pressed a button on the speaker, summoning the attention of the worker on the other end.

"Welcome to A&W!" a young man's voice exploded over the speaker, startling Emma.

"Do you guys still have that pizza burger?" Emma hollered back, looking for the word "pizza" on the oversized menu, which could have easily doubled as an eye chart in an optometrist's office.

"Yes, it's still available," he announced in a lively voice, which sounded fragmented due to the interference from the speaker's poor electrical connection.

"Sorry, I don't see it on here." She scooted closer to the car door to get a better look at the menu.

"Oh, yes, ma'am. It's in the middle of the menu, and

they spell it p-e-t-e-z-a—peteza!" The young man enunciated each letter, following it up with the pronunciation of the word, as though he were standing in front of a panel of judges competing in the national spelling bee.

"OK, I'll take one of those! Um...and some french fries, plus a large mug of root beer!" Emma shouted at the silver box.

"All right. That'll be one dollar and thirty cents. I will bring your order out as soon as it's done," he cheerfully confirmed.

Digging into her handbag, Emma withdrew five quarters and two nickels from her coin purse. Clutching the change in her left hand, she giggled like a schoolgirl, because she had taken the two nickels out, not as a tip but rather as a prize to present to the young fellow for winning A&W's spelling bee.

Before melting back into the seat and closing her eyes, she increased the radio's volume a bit to enjoy the uplifting sound of jazz trumpeter Miles Davis, as his music surged energetically from the speakers. Inhaling deeply, she drew in the restaurant's smokey burger and french fry aromas while they drifted on the breeze, making her mouth water. The seductive smell made her stomach ache. She imagined consuming a delicious ground beef patty that was grilled to what she deemed as medium-well perfection, infused with pizza sauce, and loaded with mozzarella cheese—only to be delivered on a bun for convenient consumption. "It just doesn't get any better than that!" She licked her lips in anticipation.

While visions of peteza, or pizza, burgers danced in her head, tormenting her tummy, the radio station's instrumental jazz gave way to commercials that preceded the midday news. Within minutes, a typewriter-like tone coming over the airwaves shifted the mood from happy to hopeless, as the announcer's sedate, monotone voice abruptly cut into her daydream.

"We now join our CBS affiliate in New York." The crisp, crepitate sound emitted from the car's speaker.

"This is CBS News, New York. Less than six weeks after the announcement of Senator Robert Kennedy's death, we are saddened to bring you news of another assassination attempt—this time against Minnesota Senator Eugene McCarthy, occurring yesterday afternoon in Atlanta. Only a few weeks ago, we heard the following from Senator McCarthy, commenting on the assassination of RFK..." The reporter cut to a recording of Senator McCarthy reacting to Senator Kennedy's death and subsequently announcing his intent to indefinitely suspend his political activities.

After the recording, the reporter came back on the air. "As most are aware, Senator McCarthy withdrew from the presidential race not long after this statement, but he remained active within the Democratic party, aggressively pushing the progressive side of the party's platform. It was for this reason the senator and a few of his aides traveled to Atlanta to meet with representatives from the Fulton County Democratic party yesterday. They were departing the motel where the meeting had occurred when shots rang out. CBS News learned moments ago Senator McCarthy was not, I repeat, not, struck by any of the gunman's bullets, but his cousin Patrick McCarthy, who is also his chief of staff, was hit multiple times. Both men were rushed to Georgia Baptist Hospital, and upon arrival,

Patrick McCarthy was immediately taken to surgery, as doctors worked feverishly through the evening. We are awaiting an update on his condition. This much we do know, once again an assassination attempt was made late yesterday afternoon on Senator McCarthy's life outside a motel in Atlanta. The assailant, an unidentified white man said to be in his thirties, was captured and disarmed by McCarthy's supporters, then taken into custody by Atlanta police. We will bring you more information as soon as it arrives. CBS reporters are at the hospital and police station, trying to glean whatever information they can, but none of the agencies involved are releasing any other information at this time. This is CBS News, New York."

"You are listening to 830, WCCO. We will pass along more information about the senator and his chief of staff as soon as we have it," The broadcaster reassured his listeners. "In local news..." He then proceeded with happenings from the Minneapolis--St. Paul area, while Emma listened silently.

The bouncy jazz returned after the conclusion of the news report, and her Peteza burger, french fries, and tall glass of root beer followed shortly. She had rolled the window up just enough for the young man to affix cushioned hooks, which were connected to the underside of the tray, over the glass, allowing access to the food atop it. Paying him, she congratulated him on his award-winning spelling bee performance. Initially, he appeared perplexed, then frowned comically, recalling his recital of the letters as he walked away.

There was an exorbitant amount of time left to get to the airport, yet Emma felt anxious. Her foot wiggled back and forth as she removed the foil-encased burger from the wax paper-lined plastic basket. For a moment, her foot took a break from oscillating while she carefully brought the burger to her mouth and successfully took a bite without spilling any of the pizza sauce on her clothing. Returning the heavenly grease-laden delight to the basket, she could feel her taste buds going crazy after she took a large swig from the weighty glass mug filled with draft root beer.

Grabbing the fare for another bite while still holding the mug, Emma noticed two teenagers pull up to one of the menus and exit their vehicle in favor of a hexagon-shaped table with benches attached to the bottom. Five of the wooden structures, equally spaced, formed a line down the center of the metal overhead canopy from the store front, where the car hops and the public could place and pick up orders, to the end of the drive that extended a few feet beyond the line of menus.

Summer love was in full swing, and the couple's flirtatious gestures were made known for all to see. The pair had seated themselves almost on top of one another at the table, with shoulders touching, arms entwined, and fingers toying affectionately. Initially, Emma was repulsed by the scene as she slowly gnawed on the burger and creepily stared at the couple, but then she recalled how once she, too, had been young and in love. The thought unlocked images and feelings of the attraction she'd had to Patrick. It was the type of attraction that accompanies intense insecurity, as one exposes their heart and soul to another and begins the process of creating a relationship.

The vision of the two lovers returned Emma to the question she had posed to herself earlier in the drive: When did their relationship go wrong?

Chewing over the subject while nibbling on the burger, she searched the recesses of her mind for the answer.

Numerous moments captured her attention, but one in particular stood out, so much in fact that she could hear his voice in that moment, plain as the day he said it.

"Looking for someone?" Patrick smiled admirably at Emma.

Shaking her head and swallowing the root beer-infused burger bits, Emma stirred in her seat holding both the burger and the mug as she thought about their first conversation and where it occurred.

"That dance, that stupid dance!" she exclaimed aloud, drawing attention from anyone within earshot. "That damn dance!" she continued, but this time in a more controlled manner after catching a glimpse of others watching her with concern.

"None of this would have happened if it weren't for that stupid dance," she mumbled, dropping what was left of the burger in the basket, then chugging the rest of the root beer.

45

THE DANCE

Chapter Five

❖

October 1940—Bemidji, Minnesota

Emma Dickinson's first encounter with young Patrick McCarthy occurred at the high school's homecoming dance. She was a new student at Bemidji Senior High School after her father had accepted the position as administrator at Lutheran Hospital and moved them out of St. Paul in August of that year. He enrolled Emma in the city's only secondary school for her senior year. Leaving her friends behind had dampened Emma's spirit, but she knew what the opportunity meant for her father's career and had supported it despite the personal sacrifice.

Psychologically more mature than the average seventeen-year-old she usually disliked events, like the dance. Her only reason for attending was to appease her new friend Anna, who loved swing dancing, though Emma couldn't understand why. The lofty movements involved in the choreography scared the hell out of her.

Anna DiBlasi had plugged the event since the first day they'd met in homeroom. In the days leading up to the dance, Anna bounced around school like a child anxiously awaiting Santa Claus. Friendly, charming, portly, and cheerful, with flaming red hair, was how Emma had described her new friend to her father. Emma smiled as she told him about Anna and how she would go on and on about the band, dance, and decorations, as well as how each time Anna started in about the event, she would roll her eyes and ignore the banter, convinced it was probably much ado about nothing. "After all, it's only a dance," she declared sensibly.

It wasn't until she walked through a pair of solid oak doors into the high school auditorium the evening of the event, with Anna pulling her along every step of the way, that she began to comprehend her friend's gaiety. The room had been thoroughly transformed by members of the homecoming committee. The drab hall that lay beneath the décor was almost unrecognizable, since it was camouflaged in a considerable amount of crepe paper dyed in navy blue and white. The paper cascaded from a large, elaborate metal chandelier, high above the floor and twisted its way out toward the walls. Strings of electric lights, embellished by blue-and-white globes, enhanced the aura as it followed the crepe paper and ended behind large navy blue and white bows that also hung from the walls. Confetti in long, skinny shoelace lengths, made of navy blue and white paper, danced in time with short, chunky metallic pieces of silver that floated through the air, littering the floor. Every few moments, the thud of a drum would release what remained in two canvas bags overhead, from which the majority had already escaped. Like leaves floating to earth, the lengths tumbled, twisted, and turned in the air as gravity pulled them down.

The decorations swayed to the band's thunderous drums, which boomeranged off the walls. Emma could feel the vibrations against her chest, while trombones, clarinets, and saxophones shattered conversations with a riotous explosion of jazz and swing. Eleven musicians saturated the atmosphere with sound, provoking over one hundred students to wildly spin, hop, and bounce their way across the parquet floor. Dumbstruck by the jubilant exhibition, Emma stopped instantly, breaking free of Anna's grip to take in the controlled mayhem.

As she stood in the doorway and stared, she couldn't help but feel a little out of place, if not a bit too overdressed for the occasion. The Manchester dress she wore presented a mature and more refined look, which had gained popularity among the ladies in St. Paul, compared to the plain blouses, short skirts, bobby socks, and saddle shoes trending among her classmates. Cut below the knee, the union-blue arrangement featured uniform white pinstripes running vertically along the length of the dress. A princess-cut bodice sported white, flared short sleeves of the same design. Capping off the dress was a narrow Peter Pan collar, which was made from the same white material as the sleeves. Emma nationalized the look with the addition of a quaint, red chiffon bow that was tied just below the collar, emphasizing her classic English ancestry.

The dress's waistline accentuated Emma's slender, flawless figure. White nylons hugged her legs, showing off toned calves. The red bow tie perfectly complemented Emma's blonde shoulder-length hair, which was pulled back at the sides with a simple silver clip. Everything about Emma's appearance identified her as a young lady who was always in control and knew exactly where she was going.

Dances at Derham Hall were nothing like this, she reflected, still mesmerized by the sights and sounds. Chaperones patrolled the auditorium, disrupting what they considered to be overly suggestive dance numbers. The band's tempo increased, driving the pace, vigor, and extravagance of physically exhausting moves. Emma's eyes widened as girls were wildly tossed and twirled high overhead, then safely returned to earth by energetic young men with an accomplished sense of timing. While accompanying her father to social functions in St. Paul, Emma had witnessed people performing variations of the Lindy Hop and was captivated by its energy and spontaneity, but just watching the constant spinning and swing moves left her nauseous.

Motionless, she stood watching, while the orchestra's deafening sound relinquished its command over the audience to the celebratory youth applauding the ensemble's skill. Anna reconnected with Emma, and the two meandered around the hall, stopping on occasion to mingle with different groups. Emma's girl-next-door beauty stupefied almost everyone she came into contact with, and her controlled introduction accentuated her intellect without intimidating those she encountered. Boys and girls alike enjoyed making her acquaintance and reveled in her down-to-earth presence. Connecting with other students in the youth-charged surroundings kindled a lively feeling she found intoxicating.

While there were dances and functions she attended in St. Paul where kids her age gathered, those events were tame compared to the melee she was now witnessing. Thus, encountering such exuberance was exciting. It took a bit of time for her to relax, but eventually she did, allowing herself to take pleasure in the moment. The space around her was filled with excitement as music once again reverberated off every object in the hall. The beat made Emma tap her toe and sway a bit, while she attempted to chat with others over the thunderous din.

Emma was surrounded by a group of girls when she first saw Patrick McCarthy. Caught between the crowded dance floor and some of Anna's friends, she noticed him enter the hall in the company of twenty or so strapping young men. He was remarkably built and profanely good-looking, and his appearance unleashed an energy that nourished Emma's elation. Conspicuously taller than the others, he exuded a stately, gallant stride as he led his crew across the floor. Inattentive to anyone else in the room, Emma focused all of her attention on Patrick. She watched as he drew closer to her—his dapper character accentuated by the slightly oversized suit he wore. His trousers were high-waisted and wide-legged, and he topped them off with a white button-down shirt and geometric tie. A long coat with padded shoulders completed the ensemble, and it was perfectly tailored to feature his athletic physique. The suit's earthy tone of pale brown underscored his golden blond hair, which was slicked back.

Patrick's distinctive features displayed a young man who looked to be just shy of being a collegiate. Based on his attributes and placement at the head of the entourage, Emma guessed he was a senior. He was only a few steps in front of her when he caught her staring. Confronting her sky-blue gaze, he slowed down, absorbing her glamour and statuesque beauty. Patrick would have stopped, but he quickly grew cognizant of the group following closely behind, so he continued past her, smiling confidently. Embarrassed, Emma looked away, knowing she had been caught gawking.

Assembling at the table that held a punchbowl, the group's jocularity added a buzz of excitement to the room. After momentarily pondering over why their appearance had created a stir, Emma's silent query was answered when the school's football coach interrupted the band and stepped up to the microphone. Making her way through the crowd, Emma was able to acquire a direct line of sight to the coach and a peripheral line of sight to Patrick.

The coach was only seconds into his introduction when Patrick caught a glimpse of her silhouette out of the corner of his eye. As she slowly cut through the crowd, the light from behind her had changed in intensity, alerting him to her movements. It took every ounce of self-control to refrain from looking her way. Ultimately, his curiosity got the best of him. Turning his head slightly, he made a discreet attempt at surveying her features, but the people shuffling about interfered with the effort, causing him to surrender and fully turn his head to look at her.

Emma was flawless and glistened in the light that surrounded her. He attempted to divert his eyes elsewhere while she moved, but his desire to absorb as much of her radiance as possible hindered his withdrawal. Their eyes met. Unabashed, Patrick smiled courteously. No girl had ever caught his attention so suddenly. Even from a distance, he could tell she was very glamorous. Her body language indicated she was poised, and her dress highlighted her sophisticated style. Those traits set her apart from the others.

Consumed by her, everything around him faded into a fog of noise and light. There, he blissfully lingered until chants hailing his name brought him back from his daydream. His teammates thrashed around, jostling him wildly, returning his attention to the celebration, as the coach praised his star quarterback's patience under pressure. Taking the stage, Patrick led his team onto the platform, like a conquering hero returning from battle. The auditorium shook while the band pounded out the school's anthem, driving the teenage crowd into a frenzy. The boys waved victoriously as Patrick acknowledged his fellow teammates and then the crowd with a wave of his own. Exiting without comment, he wanted to ensure the moment was about the team and not just one individual. Leaving the stage ensured the squad understood the praise they heard was for them. The applause endured for a long time, reinforcing each player's confidence in his abilities, until the collective unit departed and made their way toward a pair of doors at the far end of the hall. Patrick commended each player with a masculine high five as they passed, inspiring camaraderie and gratitude, and then he turned and trailed them through the mob.

Two athletes opened the doors, drawing the gridiron heroes out of the hall that led down a dirt path to an open area adjacent to the football field, where they religiously dominated their opponents. On this night, a bonfire would be lit to celebrate the team and the school. A cool autumn breeze had swept in through the auditorium's passage after the boys opened the doors, momentarily subduing the students' fieriness as they followed the team out of the building.

Emma lost sight of Patrick after the crowd had dissipated and filtered through the doors in the team's wake. Beginning to move with them, she subconsciously felt a pair of eyes on her. She turned around and found Patrick standing next to her.

"Looking for someone?" He smiled admirably at Emma. He was very noble in his approach, which captivated her.

"I was looking for my friend," Emma replied with ambiguity, hoping a fabrication would make her look less excited about the encounter than she really was. He could see her fidgeting with the ring on her left middle finger and doubted the authenticity of her statement.

"That's a beautiful ring," he said, exposing her angst as he tried to make conversation.

"Thank you," Emma somberly conveyed, flattening her hand and extending her fingers to look at her ring. "It is breathtaking, isn't it?" She released a heavy sigh.

"You don't sound happy about having it." Patrick searched her aqua-blue eyes.

"It was my mother's." She lifted her eyes to look at him. "My father gave it to her on their wedding day." She continued peering down at the ring and then back into his eyes.

Patrick knew nothing about her, but the melancholy response and expression on her face immediately gave a sense that something very unfortunate must have occurred for the ring to be in her possession.

"She passed away a few minutes after my birth," Emma divulged. "My father told me I have her eyes." She smiled, surveying the room. "But I think I have her smile!" Emma declared with delight, returning her gaze to his, as her dimples peaked on each cheek. The lack of activity around them enriched the silence that lingered after Emma finished. Captivated by one another, they were oblivious to the empty hall they now occupied alone.

"Your smile is exquisite," he complimented while admiring her. "Your mother must have been a very beautiful woman."

Patrick's compliment captured Emma's heart as his chestnut eyes took in her disciplined manners.

Patrick's smile accentuated his robust personality, provoking Emma to smile. Usually reserved, she believed she had shared too much, but something about him had compelled her to do so.

"She was." Emma clasped her hands and dropped them to her waist.

"Hello, my name is Patrick McCarthy." He extended his right hand toward her.

"Ah yes, I know." Emma giggled, gesturing toward the stage with a nod of her head and drift of her eyes. Confused, he turned to ascertain the meaning of her maneuver. Patrick winced as the platform came into view, and he became cognizant of the obvious.

"The coach thinks pretty highly of you." She grinned, offering her hand palm down.

"Ah... well... he ought to." Patrick joked, turning to re-engage her eyes. "I'm a pretty good player." He chuckled whimsically, grasping her fingers gently.

Emma unconsciously bit her lower lip and blushed as he held her hand in his. The warmth of his touch suddenly made her realize how chilly the auditorium had become since the doors had opened.

"Is that arrogance or confidence I detect, Mr. McCarthy?" she asked, tightening her grip to make his acquaintance.

"Perhaps a little of each, Miss...?" He tenderly squeezed

her hand in acknowledgment, then paused in anticipation of her name.

"Dickinson," she responded, impressed by his honesty. "Emily Dickinson," she continued, adding her first name.

"Emily Dickinson, like the poet?"

"Yup. But I was given my mother's namesake, not the poet's. That's why everyone calls me Emma."

"It's nice to meet you, Emma!" Patrick finally released her hand.

He was formal, cordial, and complimentary. Emma had met boys like him before, but few carried such presence.

"Would you care for something to drink?" Patrick motioned toward the punch bowl sitting unattended on a nearby table.

"Yes." She smiled broadly, and the pair made their way to the table

Removing two paper cups from a stack, Patrick filled them fractionally and carried them toward a few chairs with Emma in tow. Imploring her to sit, he waited patiently as she did, adjusting her skirt in the process. She displayed elegance in every gesture, which fascinated him. Once she was settled, he transferred the cup of punch to her waiting hands and lowered himself onto the edge of the chair next to her.

With the departure of almost everyone in the audience, members of the band finished the set, then proceeded to pack up their instruments. The absence of sound left an emptiness neither had expected. Sitting next to her, Patrick flared his nostrils as he detected a light oriental fragrance with a soft flowery scent, awakening his senses to beautiful notes of bergamot, iris, vanilla, and amber.

Silently, they sampled the punch and smiled, each waiting on the other to initiate conversation. Lowering his cup, Patrick began first.

"That's a lovely scent you have on."

"You like it? It's Shalimar!" Emma grinned.

"So, are you from around here?" He sat his cup on the floor between their chairs, then sat upright.

"Well, I guess that depends on what you mean when you say, 'from around here'?" She mimicked his voice, tipping the cup away from her lips.

"I haven't seen you in school before." He laughed at her portrayal of him. "So I presume you're not from Bemidji and have recently moved?"

"You are correct, sir!" Emma affirmed with a nod, sliding back to stabilize herself against the back of the chair. "I am not from Bemidji." She took another sip, then lowered the cup again. "But I am from Minnesota," she proudly boasted.

"So, Miss Dickinson, what brings you to this part of Minnesota?" He grinned, bending down to retrieve his drink.

"My father accepted a position at Lutheran Hospital, and we moved to Bemidji from St. Paul four weeks ago."

"Wow! St. Paul!" His voice heightened, intensifying his interest in her. "This must be quite a change for you?"

"So far it hasn't been too traumatic!" She laughed, shaking her head from side to side, stopping only to place the cup once more to her velvet-red lips. Finishing her drink, she shifted her position to the edge of her seat and stooped to place her cup where Patrick's had been on the floor. Sitting upright once more, she crossed her legs at the knees, clasped her hands in her lap, and prepared to engage him further. Her ability to roll effortlessly with the recent changes in her life fascinated him. He admired her maturity and mettle in the face of what most kids would surely consider to be an adverse event. Those qualities convinced him to look beyond her beauty.

"Actually it has been really nice," she assured him as she privately contemplated the move, the town, and the people she had already been introduced to.

"So what about you?" she prodded, eager to learn more about him.

"What about me?" He snickered.

"Are you from around here?" She smirked, once again imitating his voice and line of questioning. Her sense of humor alleviated the awkwardness still lingering in the air and made him feel at ease. Around her, he didn't have to be the school jock or hero everyone made him out to be. For the first time, he felt like he could be himself around someone his age.

"Well, I guess that depends on what you mean when you say 'from around here'?" He took her line, imitating her voice.

"Touché!" Emma let out a chortle that caught both of them by surprise, breaking the tension and causing them to laugh out loud.

As the laughter subsided, Patrick responded, "I guess you could say that I am a transplant like you." He totally devastated her premise.

"What?" Emma looked surprised.

"You didn't think your family was the only one who ever relocated to Bemidji, did you?"

"Well, no, but based upon your popularity, I presumed you had lived here all of your life."

"No, my family moved here five years ago from Watkins, Minnesota. I bet you have never heard of it before, have you?"

Emma thought for a moment, attempting to recall the towns she had visited or passed along the way to Bemidji.

"No, I haven't," she admitted, her connection to him now blossoming with the news that he was no more native to the community than she was. She knew he could appreciate the discomfort of transferring schools and beginning new friendships.

"It's a small farm town south of St. Cloud," he said, knowing she would have most certainly had to have passed through it on her way to Bemidji.

"So what led your family here?" she inquired with heightened interest in his story.

"The family business," he joked, reclining into the chair.

"And what would that be, the Mafia?" she teased, probing for an answer with a cocked brow.

"No!" He laughed. "My grandparents had settled here years ago. After my grandfather passed away, my uncle and father each inherited 50 percent of my grandfather's gasoline station. Since my uncle is more of a farmer than a businessman, he offered his share of the business to my father for half the cost. My father seized the opportunity, and ta-da, here we are."

"Ta-da? Is that your way of saying voilà?" She giggled.

"What's voilà?" He looked confused.

"It's like saying, 'and here we are.'"

"You mean like presto?" His eyebrows raised and forehead rippled, totally confused by her pronunciation.

"Yeah. Anyway, which station is it?" She distracted

58

him with a smile and changed the subject.

"Can't miss it—the Texaco on Bemidji Avenue." He scanned the hall as other kids started to make their way back in from outside. "I work there on weekends and sometimes after school."

"So you fix cars?" She looked impressed.

"Not really." He laughed nervously, embarrassed that the truth might disappoint her. "I just service them." He hoped she would understand.

"Oh, so you put gas into them?"

"Yeah, something like that." He nodded, smiling. Patrick performed other tasks around the garage but didn't elaborate further. Since Emma had never held a job outside of the chores her father asked her to complete, she found his job engaging.

"You must meet a lot of people?" Emma remarked, resting against the back of her chair.

"Sometimes." He smiled boyishly. "But most of the time, cars just pull up to the pump, I fuel them, they pay me, and then they drive away," he explained with a shrug. Talking to Emma was like taking in a breath of crisp northern Minnesota air. Most of the girls in school wanted to talk about relationships, school or social events, but she was interested in things others weren't. It was obvious she was well educated and socially adept, but he could sense something missing before it became obvious what it was.

"Do you have any brothers or sisters?" Emma queried before looking down at the floor and pondering what her life would be like if she had siblings.

"Yes," he answered eagerly. "There are two other children in my family. My brother Frank is the oldest at twenty-four. He is a mathematics professor at St. John's

University in Collegeville," he boasted. "My sister Meghan—"

"A math professor at twenty-four?" Emma interrupted. She shook her head, and her eyes widened in disbelief.

"I know it's pretty unbelievable, isn't it?" he acknowledged. "Frank and my cousin Eugene, who are only a month apart in age, used to compete with one another to see who could get the best grades in school. Anyway, it became kind of a family rivalry thing; it must have inspired them because both left Watkins at fifteen and went to St. John's Preparatory School then St. John's University."

"So what happened?" Emma asked.

"What happened with what?" Patrick didn't understand where she was going with her question.

"With their competition! Who won?"

"Neither. Each claimed to have finished with great marks and went on to graduate school, but neither shared their grade averages after prep school."

"Why do you think that is?" Emma brushed a wisp of hair from her brow.

"Not sure. I believe they both had too much respect for one another to brag. Anyway, they both teach at St. John's now. Eugene is an economics professor," Patrick responded while pondering his own future and where life would lead him.

"They both sound like very intelligent men," Emma concluded. "You said you have a sister as well?"

"Yes. Meghan is twenty." He thought about her, now out on her own. "She attends Carleton College in Northfield and is interested in German, or 'modern languages', as she likes to call it," he joked. To Patrick, his sister's studies were a mystery. He never understood her desire to learn any language other than English and failed to see a pertinent use for her education after college.

In contrast to Patrick, Emma found Meghan's choice of study timely, considering Germany's advance into Poland a year earlier. England had declared war on Nazi Germany following the invasion and had sustained aerial attacks without aid since the beginning of September. Despite pleas from Winston Churchill for the United States to intervene, American isolationists and President Roosevelt were not ready to commit the country to war.

"You seem disturbed by her choice," Emma noted pointedly. "Do we not need linguists?" She questioned his apparent agitation with Meghan's academic concentration.

"I guess I just don't see the point. What is she going to do after college?" Patrick sounded annoyed.

Emma could see he didn't feel Meghan was going to have much of a career based on her studies.

"Well, if my father is correct that the Germans will continue their advance, she may be using it earlier than we all realize." Emma shuddered. Patrick's expression to her comment reflected the collective angst of every American.

Although Patrick knew Germany's relentless conquest of Europe would eventually draw every man, woman, and child into the conflict once the enormity of the campaign was revealed, he didn't want to trouble himself with the thought. For now, Europe's war was a remote worry compared to the daily events that encumbered his world.

"I try not to think about that," he remarked, contemplating the upcoming game and his plans for the weekend.

61

Emma could see his consideration of events abroad was secondary to the challenges he faced at home.

"Who does the team play against tomorrow?" she inquired, diverting the focus of their discussion to matters closer at hand.

"Brainerd! The Warriors!" He smiled sinisterly.

The Bemidji Lumberjacks had dominated the conference over the last two seasons, and their upcoming opponent, Brainerd, bore the brunt of most recorded defeats on the lumberjacks' field.

"You seem confident in your ability to beat them." Emma was unaware of the team's wins and losses.

"How's that?" he asked, exuding the same boyish arrogance Emma had witnessed in their first exchange on the dance floor.

"Your menacing grin and the ill-boding arch of your brow." She chuckled.

"Oh yeah. Maybe so." He laughed and nervously straightened his tie, embarrassed by the ease with which she could read him. Few girls were so bold to point out the obvious, which made Emma all the more beautiful in doing so.

"You love playing football, don't you?" She noted the tip of a white handkerchief protruding from his suit pocket.

"Yes," he replied emphatically. "My dad taught me the game, and he believes I will go far. Coach Bierman even thinks I could be the Gophers' starting quarterback next year." He beamed but then stopped smiling when he didn't receive a reaction from her.

"Coach who?" she mumbled honestly, not concerned by the fact that she had no knowledge of the team, let alone the men who had stamped their legacy into the record books.

"Oh sorry! He's coached the University of Minnesota Football Team to four national championships; the most recent was last year," Patrick proudly stated, sliding to the edge of his seat as he contemplated his admiration of the coach's accomplishments.

"Oh," Emma muttered, fearing she may have lost his interest by not knowing.

"I shouldn't have expected you to know that, but I just assumed being from St. Paul and all, that maybe you would have." He shrugged.

"No." She offered a shy smile.

Patrick didn't mind her lack of exposure to the game, and he actually found it beneficial, since he could teach her about the sport. And he loved sitting beside her. Every so often, he'd catch a hint of her perfume. Tantalizing his senses, he thought once again how perfectly the fragrance suited her, which was romantic and joyful, yet not overly adult. A distinct scent, it complemented and intensified her personality.

"Sorry I assumed you would've known."

"That's all right." She immediately tried to make him feel better. "I'm the one who doesn't really follow football." As she spoke, her eyes traced the geometric pattern of squares progressing up the midline of his tie to the knot. She then added, "So this coach really thinks you are something?"

"Yeah, I guess. He traveled all the way up here to see a game last year, then invited me and my family down to tour the campus," Patrick said, energized by the prospect of going.

"But you haven't been down there to see it yet, have you?" Her face lit up as thoughts of the campus and the beautiful University of Minnesota's Armory building with its crenelated turret traversed her mind.

"No, I wanted to go immediately after the coach invited us, but my dad couldn't afford to take time away from the gas station, and despite our best efforts, we were never able to make the trip." His head dipped in disappointment. "I bet you've been there." He studied her face as he waited for her answer.

"I'll be attending next autumn," Emma exclaimed with pride.

"Really? What are you planning on studying?" Patrick was impressed to hear she'd be attending the school.

"Medicine," she boasted. "My father earned his degree in medicine from there, and I intend to do the same."

Patrick noticed how Emma sounded wise beyond her years. He then asked, "So your dad's a doctor?"

"Well, he's the hospital administrator here, but he was head physician at St. Joseph's hospital in St. Paul."

"He must be extremely pleased with your decision to follow in his footsteps." Once again, Patrick was impressed by Emma and her determination.

"He is quite excited," she concurred, recalling her father's reaction the day her acceptance letter had arrived at the Dickinson residence. Edward's response to the news was heard by all her neighbors, as his spirited celebration played out on the front porch. For weeks, he'd bragged to his colleagues about her accomplishment and regaled her with tales of his time spent as a student at the university.

"You have to go for a visit!" She shifted her legs, swiveling sideways on her seat to face him directly. "The campus is extraordinary, and the field in Memorial Stadium has some of the greenest grass I have ever seen," she conveyed excitedly, heightening Patrick's curiosity.

"I thought you said you don't really follow football?"

"I don't, but that doesn't mean I've never been to a game. My father has taken me to a few games in the Brick House," she divulged in an attempt to impress him with her knowledge of the stadium's nickname.

"Really?" His head tilted toward the floor, looking for his drink. "Think you'll come see me play there someday?"

"Maybe," she replied. "So you have decided that you're going to the University of Minnesota?" She knew her question was likely a bit too transparent.

"The #1 football program in the nation with the prettiest medical student in the land as well. Definitely! How could any other college top that?" He smiled broadly.

Flush from Patrick's fawning over her, Emma turned modestly from his view. The bonfire was fading, and students had begun filing back into the auditorium. Intense laughter announced the arrival of Anna and two other classmates Emma had become acquainted with earlier in the evening. Patrick was in the process of finishing his drink when Anna pinpointed the pair and scurried over gaily.

"Em! Where have you been?" An obvious smirk spread across her face.

"Anna, I assume you know Patrick McCarthy?" Emma gestured, leaving her seat to introduce the two.

"Of course!" Anna smiled shyly.

"How have you been, Anna?" Patrick rose to acknowledge her.

"Fine...just fine," she responded, openly staring at him.

"Patrick was just telling me about his desire to play football for the University of Minnesota next fall," Emma added in an attempt to draw Anna's attention away from Patrick.

"Huh?"

"Football?" Emma responded.

"Oh yeah. Really?" she questioned, still lost in Patrick's smile. "Wait! I heard that Notre Dame held your interest?"

"It might." He laughed, well aware of the rumors and speculation going through the student gossip chain. "But the U of M has a great football program too," he said, turning toward Emma. "And a lot to offer." He winked, then leaned in slightly to savor again the scent of her perfume.

Emma caught the inference and smiled. She was impressed that another school was vying for his attention, but she knew about his football connection to his father and how his support drove Patrick's devotion to the game. Patrick would not wander far from family or the fields of his youth.

The night was coming to a close. Anna left the pair to find the other girls.

Alone again, Emma and Patrick stood staring at one another.

"I guess I should let you go rest up for tomorrow's game?"

"Yeah, I guess so." He fiddled with the cup he was still holding. "Will I see you at the game?"

Emma shook her head indecisively and giggled. "I have never really followed football." She winked, her eyes as blue as the beautiful Minnesota sky.

"They say the grass on the field here is some of the

greenest in the state," he joked.

"Really?" She looked at his neck and reached over to adjust his tie. "I guess I will have to determine that for myself." Her hands slid down over his suit coat, then fell to her side as she met his eyes, giving him a silent affirmation that she would indeed attend the game. With a smile and nod of her head, she turned and began walking quickly toward Anna, who was now stationed by the door where they had entered from. Her stance showed that she was growing impatient.

As Emma approached Anna, she slowed her pace, trying to refrain from turning to take one last look at Patrick. She'd thoroughly enjoyed every moment she spent getting to know him and wanted to remember every detail of the evening. Arriving by Anna's side, she finally allowed herself to turn and look, but the spot where Patrick had been standing was now vacant. Physically, he had left the auditorium, but Emma felt a metaphysical connection to him, which she couldn't explain.

Anna noticed a bounce in Emma's step as they strolled down Birch Lane, making their way home. Emma emitted a fluorescence similar to the auroras that danced on the winds of the northern horizon, and her smile was as bright as a full moon on a crisp wintery night.

The two friends chatted all the way to Emma's house as Anna prodded her for details. After saying their farewells, Emma waited before leaving, as she watched Anna walk a few doors down and then disappear into the darkness of the evening. Peering momentarily toward the heavens, Emma noticed the millions of stars that blanketed the night sky. Once she was home and in her room, thoughts of Patrick continued to wander through her mind while she changed and fell into bed. As her head lay still upon the pillow, she could feel her heart thumping ardently, then eventually slowing down with fatigue from all the excitement she'd experienced tonight.

"Today was the start of something special," she thought, recounting the evening, before rolling onto her side to turn off the light on her nightstand. Happily, Emma slipped off to sleep with the image of Patrick propelling her dreams.

SOMETHING SPECIAL

Chapter Six

July 19, 1968–Faribault, Minnesota

Leaving A&W's parking lot for the interstate, Emma returned to the task at hand, which was catching a North Central Airlines—or Blue Goose as Minnesotans fondly referred to the airline—flight to Chicago at 7:20 pm. She steered the car over the road as her mind continued to reminisce about the day she met Patrick.

"The dance..." she mumbled angrily, pounding the steering wheel in a matter of fact way and shaking her head. In an attempt to drown out the memory, she turned the radio's volume up. In fact, she had entrenched herself so deep in thought that she almost didn't notice the vigorous typewriter sound coming from the vehicle's speaker, which was meant to grab the listeners' attention and warn the audience of an impending news update.

"The only thing special about that relationship was my ability to put up with Patrick's shit. Yet I did it, and still I am mixed up in it." she snapped.

The radio announcer's voice interrupted Emma's thoughts.

"This in now from Washington. Within the hour, a spokesman from Senator McCarthy's staff in Washington DC is set to provide an update regarding the assassination attempt directed at the senator late yesterday afternoon in Atlanta, Georgia. Details of the events and how they unfolded have slowly trickled into our newsroom, but we are told a McCarthy staffer should have more detailed and relevant information to share regarding the status and condition of Senator McCarthy and his cousin and chief of staff, both of whom were rushed to Georgia Baptist Hospital after the shooting. Again, within the hour, we will bring you a live broadcast from Washington DC that will update our listeners to the status and condition of Senator Eugene McCarthy and one of his senior staffers. Stay tuned for news and information."

So intently fixated on the dance and life events that had affected their relationship later, she barely even heard the information crossing the airwaves, but subconsciously noted there would be an update within the hour, so she needed to continue listening. Ultimately, it didn't really matter to her when, where, or how their relationship went bad. Her trying to find a motive was more about having an excuse for why things turned out the way they did. Despite the attempt to convince herself their relationship had been amiss from the start, deep down Emma knew the truth. She could recall the exact day and moment their lives were altered.

The last hour of the drive into the city had been more somber than angry. Emma zoned out. The Peteza burger had lodged in her stomach, making her feel very full and drowsy. Crossing over the Minnesota River, she inhaled deeply, taking in the fresh scent provided by the waterway below. The cool air rising from the river gave her a boost of energy as she passed the waypoint that most Minnesotans used to mark their proximity to the airport.

Traffic from the metropolitan area was picking up around her as she merged onto Interstate 494 East. Her heart grew melancholy when she passed the restaurants and attractions she and Patrick had visited. On the right stood Metropolitan Stadium, the iconic home of the Minnesota Vikings Football and Minnesota Twins Baseball teams. She recalled attending the Vikings first regular season game there in September of 1961 with Patrick and Carrie, who was fourteen years old at the time. Although the pair had separated, Emma had forced herself to conceal a great deal of her animosity toward Patrick, and she'd gone to great lengths to create a life as normal as possible for their daughter. Since both Emma and Patrick loved football and cheered for the same team, going to Vikings games was something Carrie could attend with her parents and observe them getting along versus quarreling. Plus, Emma wasn't about to give up her half of the season tickets they'd held since the Vikings had begun playing in Minnesota seven seasons prior.

Emma considered how football could have made their lives very different from what they'd become. For as much as Patrick loved the game and longed to be on the field, Emma had loved watching him quarterback his team, like a commander leading troops into battle.

World War II had interrupted not only their adolescence but their dreams as well. The war took its toll on relationships and lives. Ultimately, it was the war and Patrick's need to prove himself that stole her dreams.

A quick glance at the clock on the vehicle's dash

indicated she had more than enough time for a stroll, or in this case a drive, down memory lane. Giving in to temptation, she exited the freeway and made her way into the stadium's enormous parking lot. Passing small green ticket booths—set to collect payment for parking on game day—Emma accelerated toward the huge stadium. The behemoth complex had been enhanced by numerous multicolored ornamental panels hanging on the building's exterior, which had been added to give some pizzazz to the structure. The decorative elements tactfully hid most of the wide passageways that fans of the two teams used to get to their seats. Emma laughed as she recalled Carrie running up and down the wide ramps, waving triangular pennants stapled to long skinny sticks.

Patrick always spoiled her. If it wasn't a pennant, it was some other trinket. He had felt like purchasing things for Carrie would make up for the time he couldn't be near her, and he'd hoped the items would help her remember the good times she'd had with him going to the games. At fourteen, Carrie had been brassy like her father. Intelligent and a little too physically mature for her age, her fiery red hair served as a warning to her temperament, and her blue eyes were a signifier of the chill one could be exposed to after wronging her. Carrie always attracted attention and loved the limelight, much in the same way Patrick did.

Slowing the car and stopping in a front-row spot a few yards from the stadium's entrance, she placed the Pontiac into park and turned off the engine. An air bubble from the Peteza burger and root beer dislodged from her esophagus, gracefully trickling out into the air. Emma eyed the three-tier complex that was towering ominously over her, just like her relationship to the McCarthy's had for twenty-eight years. The stadium looked strong, stable, and still fairly new on the outside, but within, it had aged, as years of weathering Minnesota's seasons had taken its toll on the façade.

Opening the car door, Emma reached for her bag and grabbed the pack of cigarettes she'd purchased at the gas station then she stepped from the Bonneville. Walking to the front of the car, she extracted a cigarette from the pack and lit it. A deep inhale was followed by a weary exhale. The heels she'd been wearing since she left the house were killing her feet. To alleviate the discomfort, she carefully held the cigarette between her fingers while planting her palms firmly on the front edge of the vehicle, hoisting her derriere up onto the vehicle's hood, which caused the metal to flex and pop as it absorbed her weight.

"I know my ass is big but come on," she yelled, startled by the noise.

Adjusting her bottom, she settled in, dangling her legs over the hawk-like front of the car while scanning the stadium and reflecting on Patrick's days playing football. Though the sun floated high overhead, warming the air to a very comfortable seventy-eight degrees, the hair on her neck stood erect at the thought of witnessing his first game. "What a waste!" she concluded in retrospect, wearily shaking her head as she revived images of the talent he had been blessed with and how he'd let it go.

"I guess it wasn't totally his fault." As she stared at the stadium's colored panels, she sucked in the tar and nicotine, then audibly exhaled, pushing the smoke rapidly from her lungs. She watched the wisps of smoke effortlessly twisting and swirling about, vanishing as easily as the warm memories she had of their relationship.

Emma continued to shake her head incoherently as her mind wandered back to the first time she'd attended one of his games.

THE GAME

Chapter Seven

October 1940—Bemidji, Minnesota

Perched two rows above the fifty-yard line, Emma and Anna were privy to a great view of the field and an even better view of the sideline.

"What an awesome day." she thought to herself, taking in a breath of crisp autumn air that was impregnated with the intoxicating scent of wood drifting across the lake from sawmills. She teetered on the edge of the wooden bench seat, waiting impatiently for a glimpse of Patrick.

A loud roar diverted her attention, as the disorganized rabble from Brainerd, dressed in navy blue and gold, hustled onto the visiting team's side of the field. Seconds later a deluge of exuberance crashed down upon her, drowning the distant rumble. Men, women, boys, and girls all sprang from their seats to hail the home team as a rush of navy blue and white flooded the sideline in front of them.

Emma had forgotten to ask Patrick what number he wore, but she was sure she'd recognize him anyway. His towering personality and deliberate stride were all it took for her to recognize his location on the field, in spite of the hand-stitched leather helmet that encased his head. Oblivious to everyone around her, she anxiously watched as he prepared for the competition.

The end of an off-key rendition of the national anthem by Bemidji High School's marching band set the crowd back in their seats, while three referees in white met with the teams' captains at the center of the field. A quick coin toss decided Brainerd would receive the ball first, leaving Patrick to mull over his start on the sideline. Usually, he detested giving the other team first crack at scoring, but on this day, Patrick welcomed deferment of the ball for an opportunity to scout the stands for Emma.

The opening kickoff and lack of subsequent advancement by the visiting team were of little assistance to the star, as he hurriedly searched the stands for Emma. An aggressive Lumberjack defense strong-armed the visitors' offensive line, flushing out the quarterback and directing him into the defender's grasp. Occasionally Patrick would alter his gaze to watch as the Warriors' plays developed into disastrous passing and running attempts, but for the most part, he scoured the crowd for a glimpse of Emma, only to have his search thwarted by a fumble that forced him to take the field.

He hadn't located her, but Patrick could feel her eyes on him while he entered the huddle. Savoring the moment, he directed the play, then led his team to the line, like a battle-hardened commander. The Lumberjacks' odd formations, supplemented by Patrick's erratic cadences, bolstered confusion in the visitors' ranks. The opposing team shifted men chaotically in an attempt to anticipate the play, but the favorable field position from the Lumberjacks' defensive stance left the visiting team with only twenty yards to defend. Patrick sensed the opposition's angst and exploited their instability with an abrupt snap of the ball and misdirection play that baffled the defense. As the halfback and offensive line shifted left, Patrick tucked the ball and ran to the right with protection from the fullback. The Warriors' defense stood in awe as he barreled over the goal line for the day's first strike.

The touchdown scripted Patrick's name into the state's record book for most rushing touchdowns by a high school quarterback. Following a short celebration in the end zone, the athletes made their way to the sidelines, providing the elated group with an opportunity to congratulate Patrick on his accomplishment. Announce-ment of the record drew praise from the fans who continued their cheers and applause until Patrick acknowledged their ovation. This moment was the pinnacle of his high school career. Suddenly Emma was standing almost directly in front of him. Her allure took his breath away. Jubilant agitation from his teammates occasionally altered Patrick's view. Finally, he spotted her, and that was all that mattered. The rest of the contest was inconsequential, as the Lumberjacks rolled over their rivals and departed the field, victorious.

Following the game, it was customary for the players and students to bask in the glow of victory, or wallow in the agony of defeat, together at Diamond Point Park. The park, which sat on a sizable portion of land situated north of town on the western side of Lake Bemidji, had obtained its name by lovers who had proposed to their sweethearts beneath statuesque, fragrant pines dotting the rolling landscape. The park's arrangement also jutted out into Lake Bemidji; its layout creating a diamond formation. Near the middle of the park stood a small footbridge made of fieldstone spanning a marshy stream that drained through a narrow passage toward the lake.

Walking swiftly over a worn path leading to the bridge, Emma's pace quickened, worried that she was going to miss the festivities but most importantly Patrick.

A gathering of students in the park after a victory always created a carnival-like atmosphere atypical of the serene wilderness that offered lovers solitude. Crossing the bridge, Emma could hear the rumble of cars and chatter of people in the distance. She arrived at the parking lot around 4:15 p.m. and began to worry when she failed to see Patrick or any of his teammates. It had been almost an hour since the game ended, and she was certain everyone would have made it to the park by the time she arrived.

On her way to the point, Emma had decided to make a stop at home so she could retrieve a heavier coat. She found October in northern Minnesota to be more than a tad bit cooler than she was used to in St. Paul. While at home, she had run into her father, who reminded her of an engagement they were supposed to attend later in the evening. Adamantly, he'd requested she return home by 5:00 so that they'd have an ample amount of time to get to the event. Time seemed to fly as she wandered around the parking lot. Emma glanced back and forth from her watch to the street leading to the lot. She desperately wanted to be there when Patrick and the rest of the team arrived, but she didn't dare be late, since she knew how particular her father was when it came to arriving on time.

Fifteen more minutes passed, when members of the team slowly trickled into the parking lot. Standing patiently below the park's emerald canopy of pines, she yearned for just a moment with Patrick. Then when all hope seemed to fade, as the time for her departure drew near, he appeared.

Stepping out of a friend's car, Patrick was only able to walk a few feet away from the vehicle before he was swarmed by well-wishers. His performance and the state record had instantly made him a local celebrity, and the crowd was eager to congratulate their star.

The five o'clock hour was close at hand when Emma finally got within reach. Overwhelmed by the crowd, Patrick bounced numbly from person to person, shaking hands and smiling broadly. He had hoped to find Emma standing in front of him at each turn, only to be disappointed when he didn't. One after another, he proceeded through the group, greeting students and grinning. Exhaustion soon settled in for Patrick, as faces fused together and voices blended into the babble. His mind raced, when a sweet, singular voice summoned him back to reality. Her distinct tone captured his attention, while wisps of her perfume alerted him to her presence. Warm and welcoming, Emma stood before him, like a beacon in a sea of chaos.

Emma found it impossible to take her eyes off Patrick as light from the sun accentuated the golden highlights riddling his hair. His athletic build became more defined in the absence of his uniform and football pads. It didn't take much to convince herself he was far more handsome than the dimly lit auditorium light divulged, and she found herself totally infatuated with him. She waited anxiously to utter a few words.

By the time he was able to reach her, the five o'clock hour had passed. Patrick was ecstatic to finally see her standing in front of him. He'd contemplated what he would say the next time he had an opportunity to talk to her, and he had even practiced the words while strolling the sidelines earlier in the day, but now he stood speechless.

Face-to-face, they both continued to stare at one another, tongue-tied. The seconds flew by as they silently gazed into each other's eyes. If not for the fracas occurring around them, Emma may have never glanced at her watch.

"Damn!" she cussed, uncharacteristically.

"What? What's wrong?" Unaware that she'd been looking at her watch, he reached out to cradle her left hand, assuming she had somehow injured it.

"Oh, nothing...it's nothing," she responded, appreciatively allowing him to hold her wrist as if it had been broken. "My dad was expecting me home at five." She tilted her wrist toward him to display the time on the watch. "I'm a little late."

Patrick maneuvered her wrist to get a better look at the watch. "Ah, so you are." He smiled, returning his gaze to her while continuing to hold her hand. "I guess I should let you go then." He squeezed her hand and then released his grasp.

Hesitantly Emma allowed it to drop to her side. "Yes, I guess you should." She smiled.

Fifteen minutes had elapsed since the top of the hour, and her desire to remain in Patrick's company conflicted immensely with her obligation to accompany her father to a dinner party. Knowing what her attendance meant to her father, she didn't want to disappoint him.

"I'll see you later, OK?" she expressed confidently, backing away.

"You know it," Patrick acknowledged with a wink and a grin.

With a smile, she nodded, then turned forcefully and walked away. Arriving home only minutes later, she stood on the brick steps of the two-story home as she looked toward the park and thought of Patrick. She listened to the exuberance of the celebration, which reverberated through the pines. The sun had just set below the horizon, and she remembered how her hand had rested in his. The dreamy memory appeased her. Despite the cold, she felt very warm as her body quickly heated up at the image of Patrick holding her.

ALL IN THE FAMILY

Chapter Eight

July 19, 1968–Bloomington, Minnesota

Scorched fingers greeted Emma's return to the present. Instinctively, she threw the cigarette to the ground and furiously stomped on it.

"Damn!" Her hand shook wildly in an effort to alleviate the pain. "That's what I get for lingering too long in the past." she roared while attempting to soothe the burns and pain on her index and middle fingers by placing them in her mouth. Much like her relationship with Patrick, the cigarette she threw moments earlier still smoldered undeterred by the pounding it had received. Angrily, Emma drew a haggard breath, then slid from the hood and began walking quickly back to the driver's side. Dejected, she stood staring at the solid steel beams of the stadium while grasping the door's silver handle.

"If only you wouldn't have been so fanatical in your youth and instead were as strong and stable as that structure to have just made the break regardless of what anyone thought. Then you wouldn't be in this position."

Her voice bemoaned from within.

Pulling away from the lot, she recalled the vibrant colors on the players' jerseys, the roar of the crowd, and the thick, smoky smell of hotdogs and hamburgers that the tailgaters were grilling. The sights, sounds, and smells associated with the game of football brought an easy smile to Emma's face as the Bonneville rolled on toward the airport. Making her way closer to the airfield, Emma could feel her smile begin to diminish as her mind tussled over matters that had long been locked away.

A glance at her watch indicated she was more than three hours early for her flight. She weighed the rationale for departing the house so far in advance but concluded that her nerves and penchant for being punctual, which she'd inherited from her father, had made her leave early. She approached the exit ramp to the airport. The city of Saint Paul stood in the distance, calling her like a long-lost friend. Picturesque memories of the city from river bluffs high atop the Mississippi, which lay near to where she'd grown up, enticed her. The temptation to sojourn "home" was too intoxicating to pass up. Emma made no attempt to steer the car toward the airport's entrance as it approached. Instead, she drove on—her mind a mixture of various events, times, and places. Emma tortured herself over the years by attempting to decipher, analyze, and regurgitate every moment of their relationship, from the dance to their disassociation. Once more she allowed herself to debate the details. Even Patrick's maternal background became fodder for scrutiny and fueled her relationship conspiracy theory.

"The problem with Patrick was so genetically blatant. I was a damn idiot for not recognizing it in the beginning."

she lamented as flashbacks of Edward's polished black Plymouth arriving outside Mayor Bjorklund's Bemidji residence on a chilly October evening came to her. Anger pumped through her veins when she thought of the evening's events, which were more striking now than they had been in the years since. As much as she wanted to, she couldn't let it go. On autopilot, the Bonneville rolled over the asphalt. Emma couldn't stop herself from merging the present with the past. Physically she was driving, psychologically she was shivering while she stood outside the front door of the mayor's residence, as she allowed herself to be transported back.

****

Emma and Edward waited patiently for someone to come to the door. Finally, a woman of marked beauty opened it.

"Please, come in ... come in. I am so sorry if I left you waiting out there too long," Mrs. Bjorklund apologized profusely while welcoming Emma and her father.

"No, not at all," Edward declared. "We just arrived. Besides, it's a gorgeous evening." He detected a floral scent of rose and orange blossom with an undertone of raspberry, soft sandalwood, and patchouli.

"Well, a crisp breeze seems to be blowing in off the lake, and I'm a bit chilled even inside the house tonight." She smiled widely. "I'm Elizabeth, but my friends call me Beth."

"Hello, Beth. I'm Edward Dickinson—" he began.

"Oh, Dr. Dickinson," she interrupted as soon as she realized who he was. "It's so nice to make your acquaintance. Earl has told me so much about you." Beth attempted to restrain herself from seeming overly excited, although deep down, she was ecstatic over having a new administrator running the hospital.

"And this must be Emma?" Mrs. Bjorklund sighed, turning her gaze from Edward to Emma.

"Yes, ma'am," Emma responded cordially. She could smell the aroma of walleye, wafting from the kitchen.

"Welcome, my dear. The other young adults have gathered around the firepit, down by the lake. You are welcome to join them or stay with the adults, but we're rather boring." She laughed, waving a hand elegantly in the air.

Emma looked at Edward for approval to join the other kids, since at similar events in the past, she'd grown accustomed to circling the room in his shadow, mingling when engaged, and receiving what she referred to as a "puppy love" from the adults who patted her head and spoke to her like they would to their dogs. "Oh,... well, hi there." They would say as they leaned over and looked down at her as if they were waiting for her to perform a trick or lower her head so they could scratch behind her ears. As she grew into a young adult, their behavior became annoying and embarrassing. Though on this night, things were different. Be it a new town, time, or troop, a wink and loving smile from her father was all it took for Emma to understand she had fulfilled her daughterly obligations and would no longer be required to tail her father.

"I will show you the way if you like?" Mrs. Bjorklund offered.

"Thank you, ma'am. That would be super."

"Doctor, the men are in the living room. I'll take your

coat if you wish?" Edward had already removed his coat. He handed it to Beth. After returning from hanging his coat, she said to Emma, "Come on. Let's go find the others."

Emma nodded happily, then trailed Beth down a narrow set of stairs, through the lower level of the house, and out a rear door that opened to a sizable back yard, which was bordered by the lakefront. Beth made small talk by providing Emma with a quick history of the home and property as they walked toward a large firepit, where the other teenagers had gathered. Nothing conveyed the open air mood of a northern Minnesota evening like the woodsy smell of oak as it crackled in a bonfire. The cries of common loons wavered eerily in the distance. Small waves agitated the shoreline, releasing a pungent odor of fish in the crisp autumn air. A bouquet of leaves, which had fallen from a nearby tree, crunched beneath their feet.

Reaching the group, Mrs. Bjorklund introduced Emma, though most of those who were congregated around the fire had already made her acquaintance at school. The conversation had just begun to pick up when a shadowy figure approached from the house. Hopping up on one of the logs set near the fire creating makeshift seats, one of the boys yelled, "Hey, McCarthy, whose ass did you kiss to get invited to this shindig?"

Patrick stopped just short of the fire's fluttering glow; his face was mostly obscured by the dark.

"Probably one more distinguished than the ass you kissed to get here, Johnson!" He laughed as he walked into the light.

"I know that's true," Jack Johnson responded, springing from his wooden perch and landing with a thud in front of his friend.

"How are you doing, Killer Diller?" Jack exclaimed, shaking his best friend's hand enthusiastically while the rest of the group looked on.

"Good." Patrick chuckled. "Killer Diller? Where did you come up with that?"

Before Jack could respond, some of the others rushed over to greet him—no doubt due to his recent victory and popularity. Jack didn't mind the interruption; he had grown used to his perceived role as subservient sidekick, though Patrick never looked at him in that way. Similar to Emma and Anna's introduction, Patrick had met Jack on the first day of school after he'd moved to Bemidji. Sharing a love for football, hunting, fishing, and cars, their friendship had formed a closeness that only a trusted friend could comprehend. The boys were almost always together—in fact, so much that the kids affectionately referred to them as JP versus Jack and Patrick. It wasn't often one was without the other.

Patrick's sudden stardom had changed that a bit, since Jack continuously found himself overrun by various mobs. Standing once more at the end of the line, Emma anxiously waited for an opportunity to talk to him, while others slapped his back and marveled in his presence. Jack, now stationed next to her, laughed out loud as kids fawned over him like a movie star.

"It's really something, isn't it?" Jack sounded amused.

Emma suddenly realized Jack was standing next to her, looking at Patrick with an odd expression.

"What is?" She smiled as she asked, confused by his statement.

"Pat's sudden fame."

Jack was the only person alive who could call him Pat, since Patrick thought the shortened version of his name was too feminine.

"Hasn't he always been this popular?" Emma asked.

"No," Jack laughed, shaking his head. "Well... yes and no. Pat's been popular since the day he arrived here, due to his personality. But football has made him sought-after, which is almost worse than just being popular."

"How's that?" Emma asked curiously.

"He is popular in school. But now he's also popular in the community. Having a hundred kids following you around school is one thing; having a couple of hundred people following you around town is another."

Suddenly Emma considered the seriousness of Jack's statement. She was about to reengage him, when Patrick dispensed with the last booster and walked up to them, standing before her as he sported a big smile. He looked handsome in the wool, navy-blue-and-white letterman sweater he had donned over a plain, white lounge shirt and dark pleated khakis.

"Was your dad angry when you got home?" Patrick asked Emma.

"No, he didn't even notice that I was late because he was running behind himself. Why didn't you tell me you were invited to this?" she asked, quickly changing the subject.

"Honestly, I totally forgot about it. After the gathering at the park, Jack and I went to the station for gas. That's when my dad reminded us about the party. Jack drove home, and I caught a ride home with my dad. I really wasn't interested in the party after everything today, but I thought I would check it out." He winked.

"So you thought you would take a chance that I would be here, eh?"

"Yeah, something like that." He nodded. Hues of orange and red from the fire seemed to reflect off his eyes.

"I'm happy you did," Emma said softly.

"You look beautiful this evening. Doesn't she, Jack?" Patrick glanced at Jack, who was caught off guard while swaying uncomfortably as he tried to decide whether to slowly saunter off unnoticed or just interrupt them and announce his departure.

"Oh yeah... yeah... you look stunning," Jack agreed, placing a hand to his chin studiously, though the whole time he'd stood chatting with Emma, he hadn't even thought to look at what she was wearing and had only caught glimpses of her basic features in the firelight.

"Thank you," Emma answered zestfully, tilting her head to the side and smiling in a childlike way.

Patrick's stomach made an uneasy noise. "Have they said anything about dinner? I'm famished."

"No, but I didn't get here much before you," Emma replied.

"Yeah, I haven't had a thing since breakfast." Jack blurted out.

"Me too." Emma laughed at Jack's sudden burst of energy.

"What do you say we head in and see if they have anything to snack on?" Patrick alternated his attention between the two, then clapped his hands as though he had just called a play and was breaking the huddle.

"Sure." Emma grinned cheerfully

"On second thought, I'm going to hang out here. You two kids go have fun." A frisky grin crossed Jack's face while looking at the lovebirds.

"OK. We'll see ya in there later." Patrick slapped his best friend's hand just as his stomach grumbled out loud. Turning his attention to Emma, he motioned toward the back of the home, allowing her to take a few steps before following behind her and steadying her at the small of her back as they walked. Returning through the basement, Emma noticed a stale smell she hadn't detected on her initial trip through the area. The smell of rubber waders mingled with a moldy fish stench caught her off guard. Quickly, they moved toward the staircase that led upstairs. For a moment, their hands unintentionally bumped, then drew together as he lightly captured her fingers with his. This pleasant interaction signaled a desirable connection each had longed for throughout the day.

Exiting to the living room at the top of the stairs, Emma and Patrick noticed some of the men who had been gathered there were now making their way to the Bjorklund's sizable kitchen, where a small buffet had been set up with crepe-like hors d'oeuvres. The men began devouring appetizers made of Norwegian potato lefse, slathered in butter and sprinkled in cinnamon sugar, as Patrick and Emma stepped into the kitchen.

"Now save some room for dinner, boys." Mrs. Bjorklund half-jokingly insisted while the guys quickly depleted the tray of its goodies.

"Yeah, boys!" Mrs. McCarthy hollered obnoxiously, her slurred speech booming from the far end of a long table in an adjacent dining room. Most of the wives gathered around the table were casually chatting with one another, but Mrs. McCarthy sat alone, conversing with no one. Based upon the distance between her and the other ladies, their telltale exile of Mrs. McCarthy couldn't have been more obvious, as they passive-aggressively let her know they were less than enthused about her level of intoxication, which was clear from the stench of stagnant whiskey seeping from her pores.

Patrick winced at the sound of his mother's voice coming from the other end of the table, and he shot her an angry look. To the other guests, it was evident from the onset, Mrs. McCarthy had arrived abundantly irrigated and had made no attempt to conceal her inebriation. Upon noticing her son, she gleefully raised her cocktail in a breezy manner, dismissive of his condemnation.

"Crap," Patrick said aloud, searching for a way to escape what was sure to become a potentially embarrassing moment.

"What?" Emma asked, concerned.

"Oh, nothing. I have to use the bathroom." Patrick turned back toward the living room when he saw Mayor Bjorklund, Dr. Dickinson, and his father approaching them.

"Hi, Dad." Patrick sounded surprised.

"Here he is." Mr. McCarthy announced jovially as Emma and Patrick stood motionless before the men.

"Patrick, you know Mayor Bjorklund?" Mr. McCarthy said proudly as Patrick gripped the mayor's hand.

"Ah, yes, nice to see you again, sir. Thank you for inviting us," he answered with a nod and firm handshake.

"Good to see you again, son. Congratulations on the state record," Mayor Bjorklund gushed like a doting fan as he wildly shook Patrick's hand.

"Thank you, sir."

Patrick's father chimed in, "And son, this is Dr.

Dickinson." Mr. McCarthy happily motioned toward the doctor.

"Very nice to meet you, sir." A lump filled Patrick's throat as he suddenly felt nervous meeting Emma's father.

"I see you have met my daughter?" Edward said with a grin, shaking Patrick's hand while nodding in Emma's direction.

"Actually"—Patrick turned toward her momentarily and then looked back— "we met at the homecoming dance and have run into each other a time or two after," he joked as he brought up the evening's unexpected encounter.

"Ah, so that explains her tardiness." The doctor ribbed his daughter as his right eyebrow slanted in her direction.

"Now, Dad. I returned home immediately after the dance!" Emma protested defensively.

"I was talking about earlier this evening." Dr. Dickinson laughed, lifting a rock-cut crystal high ball glass, containing 7 Up, to his lips.

Patrick chimed in, "I apologize for that, sir. I ran into Emma at Diamond Point after the game, and we spoke at length about her desire to follow in your footsteps and attend the College of Medicine at the University of Minnesota. That's why she was late."

"Really? Medical school?" Mayor Bjorklund added, impressed.

"Yes, sir," Emma rejoined proudly. "Medicine runs in my family."

"I'm afraid it does," Dr. Dickinson added boastfully. "Emma's mother was a nurse at the hospital where I worked in St. Paul, and both of her grandfathers were doctors. Emma was accepted to the U of M last May."

"Congratulations," Mr. McCarthy praised her, giving

her an appreciative nod.

"Yes, congratulations," Mayor Bjorklund toasted her, raising his glass.

"So, Patrick, your father tells me you are quite an athlete." Dr. Dickinson shifted the focus of the conversation.

"Well, I don't know about that, sir."

"Come on, son, you don't have to be modest. It's not a crime to be proud of your accomplishment." The senior McCarthy patted his son on the shoulder, hoping his boy would brag a little.

Emma cut in for her humble classmate. "Dad, Patrick set a new state record today."

"Really? What was the accomplishment?"

"The single season record for the most rushing touchdowns by a quarterback," Patrick answered proudly.

"That's superb!" Dr. Dickinson hailed his achievement.

Edward noticed how Patrick carried himself. In build and intellect, it was obvious the boy had surpassed the majority of the young men in his class. There was nothing theatrical in his actions, and his intelligent responses trumped the athletic overtones that most would commonly stereotype him with.

"So, Patrick, have you decided where you will be attending college yet?" The mayor asked, hoping to gain an inside scoop.

"I believe so, sir," Patrick said.

"Wow! A decision." Mr. McCarthy was so caught off guard by his son's response that he almost spit his drink out.

"If you don't mind, sir, I would first like to tell my parents." Patrick looked at his father, praying he wouldn't embarrass him by pressing for more information.

"May we ask if there are any clues you would share with us, so we can guess?" Dr. Dickinson prodded.

"No clues really. But someone recently told me the football field where I want to go has some of the greenest grass they have ever seen," he toyed, leaving the trio bollixed. Silence punctuated the moment as the men pondered his answer, only to be broken by a small bell that Mrs. Bjorklund was ringing.

"Please, everyone, come and eat."

The air was rich with the enticing aromas of fried walleye and lemon, accompanied by rice and broccoli pilaf. One by one, the guests entered the dining room. Emma sat beside Edward, and Patrick beside his parents. Soon Jack and the rest of the teenagers made their way in, claiming seats around the table and settling in. They recited grace before the mayor gave a champagne toast to health, wealth, and happiness. The meal then followed with everyone happily chatting. Though the long, polished oak table was surrounded by strangers, Emma felt more comfortable around this group than any other her father had previously introduced her to. She let down her guard and casually conversed with those around her. The meal was delicious, the chocolate pudding cake dessert delectable, and the company delightful.

After dinner, the men and boys retreated to the living room, while the wives remained gathered at the table, chatting with the young ladies. Emma sat quietly as the women circled the table with talk, probing the girls for the latest school gossip and social information.

"Emma?" Mrs. Bjorklund began in a motherly tone. "Have you settled into your new surroundings?"

"Sort of; it's definitely a change from St. Paul."

"For those of you who have not met, Emma is Dr. Dickinson's daughter. A little bird informed me that she will be attending the U of M next fall to study medicine," Mrs. Bjorklund announced admirably.

"Good evening," Emma shyly greeted everyone, nodding and acknowledging each lady with a soft glance.

Most of the women answered in kind, while others just nodded in return. One woman asked, "Was your mother unable to join us tonight?"

"Ah, no, ma'am. She passed away some time ago."

"Oh dear, I am so sorry to hear that." Embarrassed by her question, the woman apologized ardently, as the mood in the room suddenly became somber.

"Oh, ma'am, it's all right," Emma reassured her, trying to recover the earlier happy mood. "Unfortunately, I never knew her, since she passed away moments after I was born."

A hush fell over almost every woman, as their hearts ached, empathizing with her. They couldn't fathom how difficult it must have been growing up not knowing the love of a mother. For what seemed like an extreme length of time, no one dared talk, but in her inebriated state, Mrs. McCarthy took exception to the issue.

"So your father never remarried?" Mrs. McCarthy asked in an antagonistic tone.

"Excuse me?" Emma replied cordially, unsure if she heard the woman correctly through her slurred dialogue.

"I asked if your father had ever remarried?" she answered in a condescending tone, as if she were talking to a toddler.

"Rose, that is none of your business." Mrs. Bjorklund snapped.

"Emma, please forgive Mrs. McCarthy. It appears she

has had a little too much to drink this evening." Beth shot an angry look at Patrick's mother.

"It's quite all right. The answer to your question, ma'am, is no. My father has never been able to let go of my mother."

"Well, I think it is a terrible shame you have been brought up void of feminine influence," Rose expelled, arrogantly slurring her words.

"Rose!" Mrs. Bjorklund countered.

Mr. McCarthy rushed in from the other room to retrieve his wife after word reached him of her intoxicated conduct.

"No girl should be left alone in a home with a man!" Rose blasted on.

"OK, Rose," Mr. McCarthy admonished his wife. "It's getting late. We should be going." He assisted her in getting up from her seat. "I am very sorry, ladies." he apologized, then hurried his wife out of the room.

Patrick stood in the doorway, looking stunned and embarrassed. He offered Emma a loving gaze as an apology. His attention was diverted when someone placed a hand on his shoulder.

"Are you all right, son?" Dr. Dickinson asked empathetically.

"Yes, sir. I'm sorry."

"Don't worry about it. You had better catch up to your mom and dad." He extended his hand cordially.

"Yeah, guess I'd better." Patrick shook his hand firmly. "Thanks, Doc."

Although every thought in his head told him not to, Patrick couldn't resist one last look at Emma. The guests noticed their attraction to one another.

For a moment Patrick paused, then quickly made his exit.

ARMISTICE DAY

Chapter Nine

November 11, 1940—Bemidji, Minnesota

Standing in the front of the high school, Emma waited patiently for her friends at the bottom of a flight of steps, which resembled a grand staircase and led to one of two identical entrances on the front side of the two-story building. Leaning back against one of the waist-high brick walls lining each side of the sweeping stairway, the afternoon sun beat down on her head, causing a bead of sweat to form on her brow and upper lip. Unseasonably warm weather prompted her to place the folders she'd been hugging against her chest on top of the wall, thus freeing her to remove a wool trench coat she'd donned earlier that morning in anticipation of a chilly November day in northern Minnesota.

Tossing the light blue jacket over her arm, she retrieved the folders with her opposite hand. She then lifted her head to search for Anne in the faces of students exiting the building. From atop the stairs to her left, she caught the high-pitched call of her friend over the enthusiastic voices coming from the exiting student body.

Stopping a few steps above Emma, Anne took an uncomfortable deep breath and watched as the horde thundered past them.

"You'd think we've never been let out early before." Anne panted, trying to catch her breath after becoming swept up in the ruckus.

"No kidding." Emma nodded, as the pair stood and watched the kids flood out of the building.

"I think we were the only school in the state that had class today. It's a holiday for crying out loud. They must've felt sorry for us and let us out early," Anne said, suddenly distracted by an excessive amount of noise coming from ducks moving erratically above.

"No." Emma turned to her. "I heard something about the weather. I guess they are worried it's going to get bad."

"Seriously? How's that going to affect the boy's championship game this afternoon against Crookston?"

"I'm not sure," Emma said.

"Well, have you talked to Patrick?"

"Not since before school." Emma adjusted her arm, which was growing tired from the weight of the coat and folders.

"Ladies," A deep voice caught their attention.

"Speak of the devil." Anne turned slightly to find Patrick and Jack descending the stairs.

"Sunbathing?" Patrick joked in a questioning manner, referencing the unseasonably warm weather, then stopped on the step in between Emma and Anne.

"Is your game still on for this afternoon?" Emma asked.

"What do you mean?" Patrick looked at her, confused.

99

"Emma heard there's a storm coming in. That's why they let us out of school early." Anne lurched into the conversation.

"Oh sure, look at the sky." Jack laughed, standing in Patrick's shadow, skeptically pointing his finger toward the sun. "Does it look like it's going to be a storm anytime soon to you guys?"

"Not really," Anne quietly answered, bowing her head and feeling a bit foolish about believing the prediction.

Defending her friend, Emma chimed in, "Jack, she isn't making it up. Seriously, that's why they let us out a little bit early."

"Listen!" Patrick's quarterback voice silenced the group. "Regardless of why we are standing here and not in class, Jack and I have a game in a few hours that we need to get ready for. As far as we know, it's still going to happen, and I really don't care whether it's sunny, rainy, sleeting, or snowing, as long as we get to beat up Crookston." He leaned forward, pounding the fist of one hand into a literature book he'd carried from the building in the other. "Anyway, I have to get going. I have to swing by the station and have my dad take a look at my car."

"Something wrong with it?" Jack asked.

"Didn't you hear it this morning when we rode in?" Patrick looked slightly behind at his friend, who was shaking his head back and forth, indicating he hadn't heard anything strange. "It's been running funny lately, and I'm not sure what's up." Patrick shrugged. "Will I see you at the game?" He turned to Emma, almost certain of her answer.

"Yeah." She nodded, initially looking at him, then averting her eyes to the sky to watch the birds dart about overhead.

100

"Come on lover boy." Jack patted his friend on the back, spurring Patrick to move.

"See ya!" Patrick winked at her as Jack's momentum unexpectantly carried him down the last step toward his car that was parked on the street in front of the school.

Descending the last few steps remaining between them, Anne stopped beside her friend and watched as the boys jubilantly made their way to Patrick's car and got in.

"I really hate Jack." A pout crossed Anne's face as her shoulders slumped. She crossed her arms in front of her chest.

"You do not." Emma turned her head and glanced at her friend with an amused smile. "You have such a huge crush on him."

"I do not." Anne stood straight up, lowering her arms and dropping her jaw wide open.

"Yes, you do. It's so obvious." Emma shifted her folders and coat from one arm to the other, dismissively waving her liberated hand in the air and shaking her head before climbing down the steps and heading home.

"I do not!" Anne repeated loudly, trailing Emma down the sidewalk, trying to convince her otherwise.

Arriving at his father's Texaco station, which was a few blocks away from the school and football field, Patrick stopped the car in front of one of the vehicle repair bays. Exiting the automobile, Patrick and Jack began walking toward the white brick structure, when the senior McCarthy met them just inside the open bay. Twisting a heavily soiled rag around his fingers and over his palms, he attempted to remove dark petroleum stains from his saturated hands while greeting the boys. A lit cigarette dangled carelessly from the left side of his mouth. Leaning back on his heels, he cocked his head sideways and lowered his chin to his chest, which made it appear as though he were considering what to say. He balled up the greasy old cloth he'd been using and crammed it into the rear pocket of his oil-soaked coveralls.

"Sounds like you need a set of plugs?" Mr. McCarthy raised his eyes and looked at the boys who'd stopped a few feet in front of him.

"Yeah?" Patrick questioned. Placing his hands on his hips, he twisted his frame toward the car to look at it. "I wasn't sure what was up with her. She just hasn't been running the same." He sounded concerned. "So I thought I better let you have a look at her." He turned back toward his father.

Pinching the cigarette between his index and middle fingers, Mr. McCarthy removed it from his mouth and exhaled loudly as he pumped out the smoke left in his lungs, then adjusted his silver wire-rimmed glasses, which were perched precariously on the end of his crooked nose.

"I don't think it's anything too serious." The older man provided an opinionated diagnosis of the problem, based on years of expertise in the vehicle maintenance profession. "But you'd better leave it here and use Ol' Red until I can get her into the shop and take a look." He tossed the cigarette to the pavement and stomped on it, knowing his son wasn't going to be thrilled with the substitute mode of transportation.

Ol' Red was a modified 1929 Ford AA tow truck that the elder McCarthy had purchased for the business shortly after he'd bought out his brother's half of the inheritance. Fire-engine red, the truck was fitted with glossy black fenders over a sizable set of front wheels that sloped back into running boards to assist passengers into and out of the Model A cab. Large round circles of pure white— bordered in black—were displayed prominently on each door and featured a five-point Texaco star of red at the center. A green "T" drawn within the star brought one's focus to the word "Texaco" which was written in black on the shoulders of the star. Just behind the cab, a formidable winch occupied a portion of the truck's bed, immediately aft of the covering. Near the back, a triangular trestle was mounted to the vehicle's heavy duty frame, just above the rear axle that extended out over the end of the truck. Both the winch and the trestle sat between two red sidewall panels that concealed the hardware affixing each piece of machinery to the truck. Wrapped consciously around the winch and extending through the peak of the gloss black trestle, one hundred feet of heavy one-inch cable was attached to a heavy metal tear-drop shaped snatch block and hook, which could be used to pull or tow another vehicle that was attached to the truck's large bumper. It sat ready for the next towing emergency.

Ol' Red didn't have the giddy up and go that most vehicles of the day had, but the truck was reliable and could power its way through just about anything that would stop other vehicles in their tracks. Patrick learned how to drive at the age of fifteen, sitting behind the steering wheel of the truck with his father at his side, providing instruction. Accelerating thirty miles per hour down an old dirt, two-track logging road would make any inexperienced motorist feel like a racecar driver circling the track at Indianapolis, but three years of driving experience combined with the superior performance provided by a Chrysler Airflow his father had recently purchased for him, left Patrick feeling less enthusiastic about the prospect of guiding the pop and sputter of Ol' Red's vintage engine over the road.

Patrick knew a slow set of wheels was better than no set of wheels, so he didn't balk at the option when his father presented it to him. The only thing he cared about was tonight's playoff game against the Crookston Pirates, who'd been the one team in the league with enough talent to challenge the Lumberjacks. The Pirates had squeaked out a last-minute victory over the Jacks, as they were known to their fans, earlier in the season while at home in Crookston. But tonight, the Jacks held a better overall record and home-field advantage. A win tonight would send the Jacks to the state tournament in St. Paul

"OK." Patrick had already surrendered himself to the idea of using the old truck.

Alternating his gaze between the two boys, Mr. McCarthy asked, "You boys heard there's supposed to be a storm coming in?"

"Yeah, supposedly that's why they let us out of school early." Jack rolled his eyes skeptically even though the sky had become overcast within the last hour.

Tilting his wrist and lowering his head, Mr. McCarthy glanced at his watch, surprised to find it was only three in the afternoon. The intense sunlight that had caused him to perspire earlier had now dimmed, allowing his neck and spine to cool off. Peering back over his left shoulder at a thermometer firmly affixed to the building's exterior, between the main door to the office and first garage door, he took note of a large white marker that indicated the temperature was forty-nine degrees. McCarthy couldn't recall what it read when he'd checked it earlier, but he knew it was definitely warmer. He scratched the back of his head, then returned his gaze to his watch.

"Wow! I thought it was later than that," he said out loud, then looked up at the faint sky. Its gray light made him believe it was close to six o'clock in the evening.

"Later than what?" Patrick asked.

"Later than three o'clock." He returned his attention to the boys. "What time is your game?"

"Four." A mischievous smile crossed Jack's face.

"I guess if I'm going to make it there in time to watch, I'd better get washed up. You know where the truck keys are?" He looked at Patrick, who acknowledged the question with a nod. "Just leave the Chrysler where it is. I'll pull it in when I'm done. The truck should be gassed up. Make sure you check the oil."

Before anyone could drive away from his station after a car repair, Mr. McCarthy always instructed them to make sure to check their oil. He didn't care who they were. He'd watch to see if they would open the hood and actually pull the dipstick to check the fluid level before they got in and drove off. If they didn't know how to check, he'd happily show them. It wasn't done to penalize people or make himself look smarter, but rather to help them. He wanted to make sure their car engines remained in good condition and running for as long as possible. Mr. McCarthy never admonished a person for not performing the check, but if they didn't, he'd make a mental note and bestow what Patrick called the "underwear adage" upon them the next time they stopped in. In his own special way, Mr. McCarthy would add the following into the conversation: "Forgetting to check a car's oil level is like forgetting to put on your underwear. What happens if your pants fail and you don't have underwear on? Your junk is going to be hanging out in the breeze."

It was a bit crass, and he often received odd looks—especially from women—after communicating the message but it worked. No matter who you were or how much of a rush you were in to get to where you were going, if you had been privy to the underwear adage, it was the first thing that crossed your mind after climbing into your car. And Lord help your conscience if you turned the engine over without checking the oil, as the adage haunted your thoughts the rest of the day.

A wink and a smile preceded Mr. McCarthy's disappearance into the recesses of the building. Patrick and Jack returned to the Chrysler to retrieve their schoolbooks, then made their way past the front of the station to the truck parked on the side of the building. Opening the doors and tossing their items inside the cab, Patrick turned back toward the office to retrieve the key, when Jack caught his attention and joked, "I'll pop the hood and check for underwear." Shaking his head, rolling his eyes, and chuckling, Patrick turned and made his way back around the corner to the front of the building.

The station was arranged so that when one looked at it from the front, two-vehicle maintenance bays made up the left side of the building, and a small office took up space on the right. Painted bright white, the building was tastefully trimmed above the doors by three equally spaced emerald-green stripes, horizontally traversing its front from left to right. Two large red stars were positioned above the stripes, equally spaced and centered over each garage door. The same welcoming green used in the stripes also highlighted the frames of the office and garage doors, as well as another large stripe that decorated the lowest blocks around the building's foundation. A large pane of clear glass exposed the full extent of the station's office to the customer looking in, and, in turn, an unobstructed view of two red-and-white Tokheim gas pumps was displayed to the attendant looking out. In large black letters, the word "Texaco" was affixed to the building, centered over the window and above the green stripes.

Crossing in front of the glass, Patrick made his way to the door that was between the pane and the first garage door, where he entered the office. Navigating around the end of an old service counter, which sat back a few feet on the right when entering the office, he grabbed the keys dangling from a silver nail placed below the counter's wooden top. Spinning them into the palm of his right hand, he turned quickly and went to exit just as the distinct double ding of a Milton signal bell announced a vehicle had pulled up to one of the pumps for service. Stopping in the door, he looked at the pumps to find Dr. Dickinson waiting in his vehicle for an attendant to assist him. Walking casually over to the car, Patrick leaned over a bit and greeted Emma's father.

"Hello, sir." Patrick caught Dr. Dickinson's attention.

"Oh, hello, Patrick. How are you?" He turned the key, stopping the vehicle's engine.

"Good, good, sir. Do you need a fill?" the younger man inquired.

"Yes, please. Oh, and check the oil also." He smiled.

"My dad's given you the speech already, hasn't he?"

"Yes." Edward laughed. "I don't want to be left hanging out in the breeze," he joked.

Just as Patrick removed the nozzle from the tall pump and placed it into the tank's filler port, the senior McCarthy approached.

"Patrick, I thought you'd left already?"

"No, was just grabbing the key for the truck, when Dr. Dickinson pulled up, so I thought I'd help him."

"Oh, hello, Edward," Mr. McCarthy said, leaning around his son to make eye contact.

"Hello, Charlie!" the doctor replied.

"Son, why don't you head out and get ready for your game. I'll help the doc." Charlie shooed him away from the pump handle.

"That's right," the doc said with interest after unintentionally catching the conversation. "You have a playoff game tonight. Who are you guys playing again?"

"Crookston," Patrick purred as though he were a cat ready to pounce on an unsuspecting mouse.

"Well, good luck!" Edward peered up at the young man, who was again spinning the ring supporting the truck's ignition key around his index finger.

"Thanks." He palmed the key once more and waved. Turning, he began to make his way toward the old Ford truck, when his father yelled, "I'll see you at the game." Turning his head slightly and throwing his hand up over his shoulder to acknowledge his father's comment, he continued to walk.

Arriving at the truck, Patrick got in and closed the door. After a cleansing breath, he relaxed into the seat by blowing all of the air from his lungs out, only to hear the sound of a sucking coming from the passenger seat as he inserted the key into the ignition. Turning his head to investigate the noise, he noticed Jack with his hands cupped around his mouth, making the obnoxious sound and giggling to himself.

"Awe, shut up." He laughed at his friend's portrayal of him "sucking up" to his girlfriend's father. Slapping Jack on the shoulder with the back of his hand, he said, "Let's go." Then he twisted the ignition key, causing the truck's engine to pop and sputter as it turned over. Pressing in the clutch, Patrick shifted the transmission into reverse, then pressed the gas while simultaneously feathering the clutch pedal. Backing out of the spot, he turned the vehicle slightly, then shifted into drive and exited the lot toward the football stadium, which was a few blocks away.

Emma and Anne stood patiently outside the football stadium's ticket window as they waited in line for their turn to purchase a pass to the game. After departing school, the pair had walked to Anne's home first and then Emma's to drop off their books. On the way home, Emma paid special attention to the low-lying clouds that had shifted erratically overhead, as hues of white, gray, blue, and black collided, like large flags confined in close proximity on a windy day. The menagerie of light and dark tones rising and descending above confirmed to Emma that a storm of some sort was approaching, and though the mass appeared to be more rain than snow-like, she went with the unpleasant feeling in her gut and kept the heavier jacket draped over her arm opposed to opting for a raincoat as Anne had. Neither girl had taken the time to change outfits, and both were dressed for the November weather in light blouses, snug-fitting sweaters, plaid knee-length skirts, white bobby socks, dark loafers, and coats. Autumn in Minnesota was usually filled with cold mornings and warm afternoons, thus the need for a jacket of some sort.

Leaves from oak and maple trees dotted sidewalks and well-worn paths leading to the football stadium. Normally vibrant in the daylight, the leaves lay washed out and crumpled on the ground, their midribs camouflaged within the faded blades, broken down by unsympathetic foot traffic. Birds continued to move oddly overhead, and an uncomfortable feeling gripped Emma when a cold breeze from the northwest began to pick up speed.

Gaining entry into the stadium, the girls made their way to the student section and claimed a set of wooden bench seats near some friends. Just as they settled in, Emma could see both teams exiting opposite ends of a building positioned just beyond the end zone to her left. The players departed a single-story building that was divided internally into three sections. Locker rooms occupied each side, and a concession stand painted royal blue with a white stripe occupied the middle of the structure. A picture of Paul Bunyan wielding an axe adorned the concession's right side, and the word "Jacks" was scripted on the other side. A thunderous roar from each aisle of the stadium greeted the young men who were racing onto the field to their respective benches.

The floor beneath Emma's feet shook from the stomping of the devoted fans' feet, only to be momentarily drowned out by deafening screams and the occasional ear-splitting whistle, as players punched and slapped each other's pads in an attempt to psych each other out before the impending competition.

Not once did Patrick look into the crowd for Emma, not even during the pep band's frosty rendition of the national anthem. His concentration was so intently focused on the task at hand that he hadn't even noticed how wet his equipment had become in the steady rain that had begun to fall, as the team's captains met in the center of the field for the coin toss. Winning the decision, the Jacks made an uncharacteristic move to receive the kick-off versus defer the first possession.

With help from a stiff wind picking up speed from the west, the Pirates' kicker launched the football high overhead and through the Lumberjacks' end zone, creating a touchback that placed the Jacks' starting point at their own twenty-yard line. Wasting little time, Bemidji's offense trudged onto the wet field and went to work without a huddle, the play already scripted. A swift snap count placed the ball in Patrick's sturdy hands, only to be stuffed into the gut of the Lumberjack's running back whose legs were feverishly churning through the wind, rain, and mud by the time he'd reached Patrick for the handoff. The offensive line slammed into the opposition's formidable defense, attempting to create a hole for the running back to sneak through, but the boys from Crookston stood their ground, quickly plugging the break in their line and forfeiting only two heavily fought over running yards to the Jacks.

The second play gave Patrick an opportunity to pass the football to his best friend and wide receiver. But it failed when Jack was unable to haul in the cold, stiff pigskin, which was thoroughly drenched in water and covered in mud, causing the ball to wobble like a wounded duck as soon as it left Patrick's hand and flew through the harsh gale.

Before the third play of the contest could be executed, the temperature nosedived instantly, turning the rain to sleet as it ferociously pelted the players and the crowd with little ice crystals. Though tiny, the crystals' jagged edges formed miniature arrowheads that mercilessly punished exposed skin. A honeybee-like sting accompanied the pointed fragments. Individuals soon appeared to be in an unchoreographed dance as they twisted, stooped, and arched their bodies to cover unprotected parts of their arms, legs, and face from the wind, which had intensified to over fifty miles per hour, propelling the crystal bits to unimaginable velocities.

The unprecedented fury sent people scrambling for cover, while damaging winds ripped a large American flag from the sturdy silver pole it had been secured to at the end of the stadium. As it flew through the air, it swept up almost everything in its path that wasn't nailed down. Without hesitation, both teams left the field for the safety of their locker rooms, which they'd departed only half an hour earlier.

Finding shelter in the women's restroom within the confines of the stadium's concrete shell, Emma and Anne stood with a few other students just inside the bathroom door. Draped in cold, damp clothing, the girls stood shivering in the unheated room as an unrelenting wind assaulted the worn door, pushing the arctic air through even the smallest opening. To stay warm, Emma and Anne resorted to hugging one another beneath Emma's trench coat. Eventually, all the ladies huddled together, taking in whatever warmth the covering and consolidated body heat could provide. A musty smell wafted about the dimly lit space. A cockroach drew the girls' attention to a corner on the floor that had been blackened by mold, which was growing at the surface of the two intersecting cement walls. Wrapped in Anne's arms, Emma chuckled at the sight of her slightly shorter friend, who then looked up at her as she pinched her nostrils shut with her fingers and declared, "I'm never using this bathroom again."

"Honestly, I just hope we live to consider ever using this bathroom again," Emma commented, her eyes stared at the ceiling and scanned the walls as the wind howled outside.

Emma thought about her father, then Patrick. On the outside, she appeared calm and collected, but within seriously contemplated her mortality and the odds of getting out of the room alive due to the frigid cold stealing the warmth away from her core. Her life with Patrick had just begun, she couldn't bring herself to imagine never looking into his eyes again.

Unbeknownst to all in the upper Midwest region of the United States, a cold air mass from the Pacific Northwest and a warm air mass from the Gulf of Mexico were violently colliding overhead, producing an intense inland storm, which had rapidly descended upon them.

The National Weather Service in Chicago had issued warnings earlier that morning, but meteorologists had underestimated the strength of the two systems. Arctic cold and gale force winds from Canada had met with warm moist air coming up from the Mississippi Valley, resulting in a bomb cyclone. Tornadoes dropped from the sky in Iowa, leveling buildings; white-out conditions from blizzards across the Dakotas stranded motorists; extreme wind, rain, and ice pummeled Wisconsin and sank ships on Lake Michigan. And in Minnesota, hundreds of underdressed duck hunters, who'd taken advantage of the warm weather and a plethora of ducks flocking ahead of the storm, were trapped in duck blinds after the sun had given way to rain, sleet, and then snow, all within an hour.

Outside the bathroom, howling winds continued the assault as the sleet changed to snow. Unsure of their next move, the ladies waited patiently for help to arrive, when muffled voices were heard yelling outside the building.

THE RESCUE

Chapter Ten

November 11, 1940—Bemidji, Minnesota

Making their way along the exterior wall of the stadium, Patrick, Jack, and a few of their teammates pushed through the blinding snow, searching the area for people who may have been overcome by the storm and had sought shelter. Unsure of whether Emma and Anne had left the stadium or were still hidden somewhere within, Patrick and Jack called out the girls' names as they led the rest of the group in a single file line, each keeping one hand on the structure and the other on the back of the person in front of them so that they wouldn't lose one another.

The boys had used a fence, which circled the field, as a reference point to aid them in getting to the bleachers. Fatigued and freezing from fighting the wind and snow, Jack and Patrick did the best they could to belt out the girls' names, but the moment they opened their mouths to call out, the air entering their lungs was so cold that it hurt to speak.

When Anne first heard Jack's muffled voice calling her

name, she deduced it was probably just her mind shutting down due to the cold. "The freezing temp must be going to my head." She dismissed the thought that her crush would even consider coming after her, or even think of her, but then she heard his breathless voice calling her name again.

"Did you hear that?" Anne shuddered.

Initially, Emma shook her head. She couldn't hear anything other than the wind brutally jostling the bathroom door against its frame, but as the boys drew closer, she began to pick up the faint sound of male voices hailing their names between the wind's intense fluctuations.

"I do now," Emma whispered, tilting her head toward the door to see if she could hear the voices again.

"We're in here!" Anna yelled, shaking uncontrollably, praying the boys could hear her tremulous voice over the low hum that was being generated by the cyclone as it whipped its way around the stadium and through the trees. A bang on the exterior of the door was closely followed by a blast of frigid air, as Patrick, Jack, and the players following him broke through a layer of ice that was weighing down the panel enclosing the aperture.

Brushing frozen precipitation from their faces and brows, their eyes adjusted to the dim light coming from a single bulb that was dangling over the center of the room. Their eyes landed on the girls huddled together in the back corner. Rushing to their sides, Patrick could see a faint smile cross Emma's icy-blue lips, as her teeth chattered wildly and her body trembled involuntarily. Although Emma and the other girls were chilled, Anne was by far in the worst condition. The boys had removed their bulky shoulder pads and had put their jerseys back on before making their way out into the storm to look for people. Noticing Anne's deteriorating condition, Jack removed his jersey, leaving the T-shirt he'd worn under his pads as his body's only line of defense against the harsh conditions. Without hesitation, he wrapped it around Anne, then took her body into his arms, cradling her akin to a groom carrying his bride over the threshold. Cold and fatigued, Anne crossed her arms over her chest. Her legs dangled freely, while her head rested on Jack's shoulder. Their eyes met.

"I've got you, pretty lady." Emma heard Jack whisper affectionately into Anne's ear, revealing feelings for her he hadn't before. Relaxing a little, Anne swallowed forcibly and closed her eyes. Covering her with the coat the ladies had been huddled under, Emma tucked the edges of the wool jacket around her friend, then turned to Patrick, firmly hugging him and placing a kiss on his lips. Though his lips were cold due to the conditions, the exchange gratified her heart, as he hugged her tightly. It was the first time the two had shared a kiss, and despite the icy circumstances, an effortless warmth consumed her as he released his hold on her a bit and looked lovingly into her eyes.

"You didn't think I was going to leave you out here to die, did you?"

"Well, I wasn't sure you even knew I was at the game." Emma tilted her head slightly as it nuzzled against Patrick's chest.

"I knew you were there. I could feel you." Patrick gave her a loving little smile.

Turning to the others, he called out. "Is everyone OK?"

117

"Yes," someone mumbled. The others just nodded wearily. It was apparent some of them were entering the initial stages of hypothermia.

"We need to get to the locker room; there's heat there," Patrick informed them. The water vapor from his lungs condensed into a mist in the air as he spoke. Assembling the group into a makeshift circle, he leaned in and told them of his plan.

"You can't see anything outside, so we need to stay in a single file line along the wall. I'll lead the way, and I want boys and girls alternating in line and holding hands. The wall will lead us to the fence, which will take us to the other building." He drew in a deep breath. "Stay together. You guys got that?" Patrick searched their eyes. All acknowledged with a nod, then lined up as directed.

Still cradling Anne in his arms, Jack asked her if she thought she could walk.

"Yeah," she muttered, thoroughly exhausted. But her jaw tightened, for she was determined to at least try. Slowly Jack released her legs and guided her feet to the floor. Once upright Anne let go of him and tried to steady herself. Looking as though she were making her first attempt at standing on ice skates, she hunched over. Her stance was wide, and her arms were out in front of her as she kept her eyes straight ahead. Teetering back and forth, she tried to maintain her balance. Her head spun while her hands begin to tremble, then she fell forward. But Jack, who was now holding Emma's coat that had been covering her only moments earlier, caught her before she could topple over.

"Let me help you," he said affectionately, supporting her. "Hold on to me while I put the coat on you," he added.

Anne closed her eyes, then gripped his waist tightly to further steady herself. Calmly he maneuvered her arms into the sleeves, pulled the coat over her shoulders, then aided her in buttoning it.

"Hold my hand tight, OK?" He gave her a firm glance, which her ashen face acknowledged with a smile.

"Everyone ready?" Patrick called out, taking Emma's hand in his. "All right? Let's go!" Exiting the door, he turned to the right. Emma, Jack, Anne, and the rest of the group followed, holding hands as they went along. As soon as they were exposed to the glacial zephyr, their breath was taken away, and each gasped for air, fighting the icy brutality pushing them up against the wall they were using to navigate. Undaunted, Patrick and the rest of the group moved forward through the knee-deep snow that was collecting in a drift along the building. The cold wind made the teenagers' eyes water profusely, blurring their vision. Numbing snow chilled the girls' bare legs to the bone and filled up the space between the interior wall of their shoes and bobby socks.

Though the wind continued its assault, snow falling from above had let up just enough for them to see a few feet further ahead than the boys had been able to when they'd left the locker room in search of the people stranded. Large snowdrifts, piling up around them, grew bigger by the minute, as the wind moved the white powder over the earth's surface. Between the gusts, Patrick was able to ascertain obstacles roughly five to ten feet ahead of the group. Arriving at the chain-link fence that was anchored to the side of the grandstand, Patrick paused to ensure he hadn't lost anyone along the way. After everyone was accounted for, he gripped the top of the four-foot barrier and trudged on through the snow, cutting a path for others to follow. The wind stung Emma's face, and she couldn't recall a time in her short life when her body had felt so frigid and numb. As she slogged behind Patrick, her feet met the uneven ground beneath her, as though they were weighty blocks of ice cut from Lake Bemidji by ice harvesters. She struggled to maintain her grip on Patrick's and Jack's hands and thanked God they were strong enough to keep their hold on hers. On occasion, the staunch wind would drive the line of students into the metal chain-link fence that surrounded the stadium's grounds. The fence extended on one end of the stadium from the home team's grandstand, around the end of the field, past the flagpole, to another cement grandstand, which was meant to host the visitors' supporters. On the opposite end of the stadium and each of the grandstands, the fence wrapped around the field, only to be interrupted by the building containing the locker rooms and concession stand. A walk that normally took only two minutes in nice weather now was over twenty minutes, due to the driving snow.

Reaching the door, Patrick burst into the room, pulling the group with him toward the warm space. As they floundered through the opening, the wind nipped at their backs. The last two boys in line hurried to shut the door before the intense cold could invade the area. Landing in a heap atop a rubber mat that covered the floor, the girls coughed and gasped for air, as each struggled to catch their breath in the damp and musty space. Dimly lit, the room was cluttered with football equipment that was haphazardly strewn everywhere. The place lacked character. If not for the black rubber mat, unpainted brick walls, pale yellow pine lockers lining the barrier to the outside of the building, and straight grain benches of the same wood and color sitting in front of the lockers, the space wouldn't have any sort of distinctiveness.

The naturally-stained, handmade pine lockers, stood at five and a half feet. Each locker reflected a lumberjack craftsmanship distinct to the men who had logged northern Minnesota's forests. A three-panel door adorned by a tarnished silver knob and five holes that bored into the pattern of a cross through the upper quarter of each panel, provided access and ventilation to each of the vertical chests. Fragrant pine, which had once pervaded the room, had long since vanished. The space was now overrun by the stench from sweaty pubescent boys.

Reaching in, Patrick helped Emma to her feet, while Jack tended to Anne. Some of the boys who'd remained in the locker room assisted the other girls. Jack, Emma, and Patrick accompanied Anne to one of the worn wooden benches that were spaced a few feet in front of the lockers. Taking a seat on the bench ahead of her friend, Emma momentarily glanced at the faces of the others gathered in small groups around the room. Teenagers huddled on a bench on the other side of the entry she'd just used to access the building. She could hear boys in the group reminiscing about their harrowing experience of departing the stadium, as though they were soldiers who'd just returned from combat. The women who had congregated in a corner were chatting energetically about how the men should be creating a plan to get them home. The men were gathered behind them, standing in front of the open doorway that led to the bathroom and showers. They reflected on the number of ducks they'd seen in flight overhead. One of the men became animated as he pretended to point a shotgun into the air and shoot, as the others commented on what good hunting they'd probably missed out on by attending the game.

Emma wrapped her right arm around Anne, who was shivering uncontrollably, then grasped her left bicep with the other hand to support Anne's frame, while the boys knelt in front of her to assess her condition. She appeared drowsy and uncoordinated. Rubbing Anne's arms, Emma could feel the morbid cold fighting to retain its hold on her. Her skin had become red in some areas and bluish-gray in others—primarily on her ears and the tip of her nose.

"We need to get her to the hospital!" Jack exclaimed.

A confused look crossed Emma's face. "Jack, come on. How are we going to do that? We could hardly get from one building to the other!"

"Look at her! We have to!" Jack's fear was evident in his voice as he stared into Emma's eyes before rising to his feet. Rubbing his hands together, he began pacing as he considered his options.

"I have my dad's truck," Patrick said softly, lowering his eyes to the floor, then lifting them to connect with Emma's.

"So?" She shrugged, certain the boys had lost their minds if they seriously considered going back out into the storm.

"It's a tow truck," he said in a very matter of fact tone. "That truck weighs more than probably any vehicle on the road around here and can go through just about anything." He stood, sighed heavily, then crossed his arms while explaining the vehicle's capabilities. "We'd have to cram all four of us into the cab, but we could get her there."

"That's the craziest idea I have ever heard." Emma's heart began to race at the thought of getting stranded in the storm. "It's frostnip. All we have to do is warm her body and she'll be fine." She made an attempt to convince herself.

"Em, it's worse than that and you know it. She's bordering on hypothermia." Patrick's eyes looked calm and resolved to the task.

The thought of dragging Anne back outside into the storm, then attempting to drive to the hospital only a few city blocks away, didn't sit well with Emma, yet she knew her friend needed attention. Though she couldn't pinpoint the reason, Patrick's absurd desire to brave the storm comforted her slightly, and she knew he was right. Emma could see the determination in the slant of his brow, confidence through the depth of his gaze, and courageousness in the sturdiness of his jaw. All of these traits only gave a glimpse to the adrenaline-charged core within him, which scared the shit out of Emma, yet made her feel indestructible while in his presence. Her muscles stiffened as she closed her eyes and drew in a deep, burdened breath before she exhaled forcefully and turned her gaze to him.

"OK," she responded. "What's your plan?"

WINDS OF CHANGE

Chapter Eleven

———❖———

Dec 22, 1940—Bemidji, Minnesota

Sitting quietly on a wooden bench just inside the narthex, Patrick hunched forward, placed his elbows on his knees, and clasped his head in his hands. He watched his toes flex beneath the top of his patent leather dress shoes before he wiggled them. Taking a deep breath created a momentary constriction around his athletic chest, which was only made worse by the tight-fitting suit coat he'd donned for the occasion. Exhaling forcibly, a few strands of his lightly oiled locks dangled loosely over his forehead to reveal a horseshoe-shaped wrinkle between his eyebrows—a clear sign that he was troubled.

Lifting his head, he raised his eyes to find a kaleidoscope of color speckling the floor in front of him, as the sun's warm light filtered through a stained glass window behind him.

"What's the matter?" Jack shifted his seat a little to give his friend more room on the narrow pew they shared.

"I hate waiting."

"Yeah. You've never been very patient." Jack reclined back and crossed his ankles. Folding his arms over his chest. Closing his eyes, he repositioned his shoulder blades against the wooden backrest.

"What does that mean?" Patrick lifted his head from his hands and turned slightly back.

"Well...you remember that play in the second quarter of that game against Crosby?"

"What play?"

"The one just before halftime. You threw the ball to Peterson for the gain of four yards."

"Yeah, so?"

"Well, had you waited a few seconds, I would have been open in the end zone." Jack opened his eyes slightly to observe Patrick's reaction.

"Awe bullshit." Patrick leaned back, extending his legs out in front of him and crossing his arms in front of his chest as Jack had.

"It's true. Your pigheaded desire to make something happen quickly versus patiently waiting for the play to fully develop has been your Achilles' heel," Jack conveyed in a matter of fact tone.

Patrick chuckled. "And your inability to hold on to the ball has been yours." He shut his eyes before adding, "We won the game and the championship, didn't we?"

"I'm not doggin' ya. Just pointing it out so that when you become a snooty college quarterback, you'll think about it."

"Snooty college quarterback?" He opened his eyes, then snickered just as one of the church's double doors swung open, surprising the boys.

Quickly rising to their feet, the boys stood in front of

the pew, as Mr. and Mrs. DeBlasi entered. They were followed closely by Dr. Dickinson and Jack's parents. Patting Patrick on the back, Jack grinned, then followed his mom, dad, and the DeBlasis down a nearby stairwell leading to the church's basement.

"Hello, sir," Patrick greeted Edward, who'd momentarily paused while allowing the others to go ahead of him.

"Hello, Patrick." The doctor blinked erratically, his eyes adjusting to the dark church interior. "Have you been downstairs yet?"

"No. Jack and I just thought we'd better wait for everyone before we went down.

"Where are your parents?" The doctor searched the area to ensure he hadn't missed them.

"My dad had to work, and my mom's at home doing housework." Patrick rubbed his forehead, certain the doctor could see through his story as it pertained to his mother's whereabouts.

"I see. Well then, I guess we should make our way to the basement." He gave Patrick a knowing glance and motioned toward the stairs.

Descending the last step of the staircase, the men arrived in the church's sizable basement. There were numerous families from the community. Some were already seated in chairs, while others were moving toward the empty chairs that sat neatly arranged around large, circular tables. Claiming two chairs next to Jack and his parents, Patrick and Edward settled in, when a chorus of young ladies at the front of the room began to sing "O Holy Night."

Standing energetically in the middle of the back row, Emma and Anne harmonized with eighteen other girls.

The congregation took notice of the ladies' angelic voices, which blended beautifully into a single psalm and bounced off the basement's white block walls, as they celebrated the birth of Christ.

Though Christmas was still a few days away, the psychological and physical strife that Bemidji's residents had overcome just in getting to this point were the best gifts any of them could have wished to receive. Earlier in the year, heated debate had ensued between the isolationists and the interventionists regarding US involvement in the war in Europe. By the time October had arrived, a bitter political squabble had gripped the nation and community over presidential candidates Franklin D. Roosevelt and Wendell Willkie. Though the election on November 5th had given Roosevelt an unprecedented third term, a great deal of animosity and division still lingered, until the Armistice Day Storm—six days after the election—had brought the citizens together again.

Thanksgiving Day was a moment in which the residents of Bemidji were truly thankful for their liberty and lives. And with Christmas now so close, many felt as though they'd been reborn. So it was with that sentiment that members of the First Presbyterian Church gathered in the building's basement to celebrate the birth of Christ.

Gazing into the audience from her perch, Emma was elated to see her father and Patrick seated beside one another while she performed. She was also euphoric over the opportunity to stand once again beside her best friend as they sang with the choir. Offering her left hand to Anne, she gazed admirably at her friend, who reciprocated the look, then did the best she could to hold on to Emma's—for she no longer had her ring and pinky fingers. Exposure to the arctic cold from the blizzard had damaged the tissue so severely on a few of Anne's uncovered fingers that the extremities had to be removed. She'd spent the following week recovering from her surgery with Jack attending to her as much as the hospital's strict visiting hours would allow.

After the storm, members of the community did their best to clear snow from the streets and drives. Although many of the roads were impassable to the average vehicle, Patrick was able to maneuver Ol' Red around town to assist those who'd abandoned their automobiles and sought shelter elsewhere after their cars had become trapped in the sudden storm. Patrick eventually helped Edward free his drift-entombed car from the hospital's snow-covered parking lot, then towed it to the Dickinson's home, where he, in turn, cleared the driveway of snow. The storm had deposited so much snow over the area that winds were able to whip the powder into drifts high enough to cover some train cars from top to bottom at the rail yard.

Following the choir's performance, women from the church began herding attendees toward the buffet they'd arranged for the event. Several families contributed their favorite dishes to the occasion. Two long tables were packed with trays and bowls consisting of mashed potatoes and gravy, coleslaw, cranberries, green bean casserole, tater tot hot dish, goulash, turkey, ham, and even a pan of lutefisk—though the smelly fare sat noticeably untouched near the end of the table and beside a stack of rolled lefse, which was surrounded by sticks of butter and bowls of brown-and-white sugar.

Joining Patrick and her father in line, Emma listened

to the idle chatter circulating around the room. She sniffed the air, absorbing the aromas wafting from the various platters. The flicker of candles centered on each table cast a warm glow throughout the room, which was decorated in red, green, and white. A Christmas tree adorned with soft white lights and simple ornaments, which had been crafted by Sunday school children, occupied one corner of the room. A manger scene portraying the birth of Christ was displayed in another corner.

After most of the guests had finished dinner, they were engaged in lively conversation, when a man dressed as Santa Claus came bounding down the stairs, towing a sack full of toys for the kids. The calm morphed into mayhem, as children of all ages rushed the man with exuberant cheers and bright smiles. Emma was laughing at the cuteness of it all, when Patrick leaned over, took her hand in his, and softly whispered, "I love you" into her ear. It was the first time he'd disclosed his intense devotion to her, and she affectionately answered, "I love you too." Though a kiss was inappropriate at that moment, given their public surroundings, they stared deeply into each other's eyes. Emma couldn't have imagined a more perfect afternoon of fellowship, until Patrick said, "So, there's something I have to tell you." His eyes lowered to the floor as his face grew somber.

"Yes?" Emma's eyes widened, and her eyebrows elevated slightly, anticipating the worst.

"My father is Santa Claus." He tapped his foot and clutched her hand tightly, lifting his gaze to meet her fearful look.

"What?" Emma's forehead wrinkled, and her eyes narrowed as she searched Patrick's expression for more information.

Patrick pointed at the man in the red suit, his face becoming flushed as embarrassment made him once again lower his head. "My father is Santa," he repeated.

Turning to see what he was pointing at, Emma lifted her hand to cover her open mouth after it suddenly became evident that the man dressed as Santa was Patrick's father.

Returning her gaze to Patrick, she giggled. "That's cute."

"It isn't cute; it's embarrassing. That's what it is."

"I think it's adorable. Look at the smiles on the kids' faces!" she exclaimed, subsequently searching the room, curious as to where Patrick's mother was. "Where's your mom?"

"That's an even more embarrassing part."

Before Patrick could even provide an answer, Mrs. McCarthy boisterously bounded down the stairs, dressed as Mrs. Claus. A bag of candy canes in one hand and a large drink in the other, it was obvious there was more in the cup than just hot chocolate. Unable to watch his mother make a mockery of herself, Patrick excused himself from the table and made his way upstairs to the sanctuary where Emma eventually found him, quietly praying.

"Hey," she greeted him, announcing her presence, then took a seat beside him. "Praying for a new car?" she joked.

"No." He snickered and let out a heavy sigh. "The alcohol is killing her," he somberly admitted. "I can see the difference in her a little more each day."

"Yeah?" Emma answered, not knowing what else to say.

"She's lost a lot of weight, attempts to cover the

yellowing of her skin with makeup, and bleeds from her mouth from time to time." He looked at her while fiddling with his fingers. "The worst part is the anger and abuse. She gets so mean." His head tilted. His face looked clearly distressed by the situation and the certainty of the inevitable outcome that would befall his mother. On numerous occasions, Emma had been the recipient of Rose McCarthy's verbal abuse. Just calling the McCarthy home held a potential for conflict, as her foul and all too intoxicated mouth belittled anyone who dared to contact a family member.

Sliding closer to Patrick, Emma grabbed his hand and placed her head on his shoulder. Staring at a large statue of Jesus behind a white marble altar, the pair sat silently praying for answers and searching for a solution. Less than six months later the sum of his fears materialized when his mother was found one morning deceased in her bed. After the funeral, Patrick vowed never to consume alcohol the way his mother had, but things change and so can those with the best of intentions.

GHOSTS

Chapter Twelve

July 19, 1968–St. Paul, Minnesota

Other than a partial view of St. Paul and the Mississippi River through several large trees, there was nothing special about the yellow, stucco, two-story home that sat high atop the bluffs on Cherokee Avenue.

"Nothing special except that this is the place where my life began and my mother's ended," Emma reflected, pulling the Bonneville to the curb directly in front of the home, then stopping. The house hadn't drastically changed over the last twenty-eight years except for the color. Everything else was identical as the day she and Edward had closed the front door and departed for Bemidji.

"My God! That awful sun-yellow color has got to go!" She squinted, turning her head to look at the house while placing the car in park. "Who would do that to such a beautiful house?" Her head shook in wonder. Since her maternal grandparents had resided only a few blocks away, Emma had become accustomed to making her way past the house, bathing in its nostalgic ambiance, whenever she visited them. During her time at the University of Minnesota, the house had become a shrine of sorts in which she felt an obligation to make a pilgrimage on her birthday and holidays. When given the opportunity, she would sit across the street and visually walk through the home's four-bedroom, one-bath interior. The last ten years or so had been the exception. There had been too much happening in her life, and since both of her grandparents had passed away, there was no reason to journey past the house, other than the occasional visit to friends who still resided in the area. But she was no longer as close to those friends as she once was.

"How does the time fly by so fast?" she wondered, studying the landscape. A northern white cedar tree in the front yard brought visions of when she and Edward had decorated it for the holidays. The tree now stood twice the height it did back then, but Emma could visualize herself loading it up with lights and ribbon. Christmas always held a very special place in her heart, primarily because of how her father was so giddy during the season. The house was always decorated with strands of red-and-white lights, which brightly illuminated the porch. The candy cane colored lights wrapped around the posts and railings. The house was also decked out in bows and ribbon. Her father would bound around the yard, decorating like a kid experiencing his first Christmas.

One of her last happy memories with Patrick was during the Christmas of 1940. After the Armistice Day Blizzard in early November of that year, she and Patrick had grown closer than ever. For Emma, a new town, friends, and relationship had made Christmas that year even more festive than any she could recollect. Even a quick Christmas Eve dinner with the McCarthys had gone off without incident, though a slight tension had hung heavily in the air because of Rose's intoxicated rant back in October. It was the only time throughout the rest of their relationship and Rose's life that she had managed to hold her intoxicated tongue.

"That woman was a work of art." She paused, her gaze slowly wandering over the sidewalk that led to the front door of the house, as she reflected on her mother-in-law's short life.

"Cirrhosis is a bitch!" She chuckled, when suddenly her peripheral vision caught a movement to her left.

"May I help you?" The sound of a powerful voice boomed over to her.

"Oh!" Emma gripped the steering wheel, surprised by the police officer's presence.

"You all right?" The burly, dark-haired gentleman questioned in a thick accent. "I noticed your car has been parked here for a while, and you hadn't exited, so I thought I would see if everything was OK." His eastern accent was now more obvious.

"Oh... oh yes." Emma nodded while releasing her staunch grip on the wheel, easing herself back into the seat.

"I just stopped to look at that house." She pointed, her finger angling in the house's direction.

"That house?" The officer nodded in the same direction.

"Yeah, the god-awful sun-yellow one." Emma giggled. "I used to live there," she added, noticing a strange look cross the officer's face.

"That's my house!" The officer pointed out proudly.

"Oh... ah... well... sorry!" She clenched the wheel again, embarrassed by her insensitive comment.

"Nah, don't be!" His thick New England accent came out even more prominently than before.

"Me and the Mrs. just moved here from Boston. Took a job with the Saint Paul Police. She loves the house, even the color. I prefer something a little more blue, ya know? But what can I do? She's happy with it, so..." He chuckled in a hearty tone.

"Uh-ha!" Emma nodded and grinned.

"So, you used to live here?" He pleasantly made conversation.

"Ah... yes, yes. About twenty some years ago." She stared at the car's hood.

"Wow! I bet it sure was a beauty back then. So, the previous owners told us there's a ghost in the house. Says she rearranges stuff from time to time. You know anything about it?" the man inquired.

"Meh ... not really." Emma shook her head but then looked directly at him and asked, "How do you know it's female?"

"The ghost? I don't, just the way they was talkin'." The policeman crossed his arms and shifted his weight to his heels. "They say things in this one room tend to move from place to place." He pointed toward the room on the front side, upper level of the home.

"First room on the second floor?" Emma asked.

"Yeah, that one! How'd you guess?"

"Interesting." She swung her head toward the house, searching the windows for movement after the man confirmed something she'd suspected all along.

"How so?"

Emma turned her head back toward the man. "My mother died giving birth to me in that room," She answered in an almost businesslike tone, stunning the man. "The ghost's name is Emily," she added, tilting her head, then pressing the brake and shifting the Bonneville into drive. "I wouldn't worry about her though. She's harmless. Just looking for her stuff, I'm sure." And with that, Emma smiled, shrugged her shoulders, and rolled away from the curb, leaving the dazed man to mull over the information he had just attained.

Her return to the airport was anything other than direct. A drive down Cherokee Avenue to Annapolis Street brought her near Saint James Lutheran Church, where she and her father had worshipped. A left turn on Annapolis led her the rest of the way to Riverview Cemetery, where she stopped for a few minutes on a hillside that was enhanced by large granite headstones bearing the surnames Bowes and Dickinson. She sat, quietly staring at the markers from her car, praying she wouldn't have to return to the cemetery anytime soon to bury her aging father. Edward was still very active, but getting on in years, and she couldn't stand the thought of losing him. Leaving the burial grounds, she once again reflected on the remainder of her senior year at Bemidji High School and the great times she and Patrick had at Diamond Point Park.

Arriving in the parking lot across from the terminal, Emma released a heavy sigh and thumped her head against the vinyl headrest. Shifting her gaze toward the terminal, she could see the iconic white, jagged metal roof covering the building. Near the middle of the two-story structure, large black-and-silver block letters called out the airport's name: Minneapolis-St. Paul International Airport.

Lifting her head from her makeshift pillow, she grabbed her purse and retrieved another cigarette from the pack. Placing it in her mouth, she fired up the vehicle's cigarette lighter. "God, I hate flying!" she mumbled, the stick dangling from the side of her mouth. Soon the car's lighter popped, and the hot, red, glowing coil put flame to paper. Inhaling deeply, Emma could feel her lungs filling with the tar and nicotine then a heavy exhale emptied them of smoke. She relaxed back into the seat.

Despite Emma's hatred of flying, she loved going places. She felt fortunate that she earned a lucrative income from her career as a physician, which allowed her to travel to foreign lands and experience different cultures. Emma loved airports and believed terminals to be exquisite tributes to man's evolution in transportation. Based upon the late President Kennedy's challenge to put a man on the moon, she didn't rule out the possibility of someday boarding some sort of super airplane at one of these terminals. She hoped the vehicle would not be so cumbersome to board and rough to fly in, since she found the current state of air travel too arduous and turbulent.

"One hour to go before takeoff," she acknowledged, snapping her wrist sideways to view the face of her watch. "Guess I had better get going."

Flicking the hot cigarette butt out the open window, she left it to smolder on the ground, then shoved the cigarette pack into her purse and rolled up the window. Engaging a switch, she returned the convertible top to the closed position, then opened the Bonneville's door. Exiting the car, she ensured her dress and blouse were in place and unwrinkled before pressing down on the silver, plastic mushroom-shaped lock knob. Locking the door, she switched from a square to a round metal key on her keyring and walked to the trunk. Inserting the key into the compartment's locking mechanism, she twisted it, releasing the latch. She took out the only piece of luggage she had brought and placed it on the blacktop by her feet. Closing the trunk's lid required a bit more effort to ensure that the chamber was secure after slamming it shut.

Stooping slightly in her heels, Emma lifted her luggage and began heading toward the building. The putrid smell of car engine exhaust mingled with the sweet chemical scent of refined jet fuel, saturating the air. In the distance, the high-pitched whistle of a jet engine drowned out the buzz of another plane's propeller, which was rotating to a start. Together the two sounds brought to mind Memorial Stadium on the University of Minnesota's campus and the midrange roar of the crowd on a bright autumn day. The various types of sonance reverberating off the terminal building elicited an anxious thump in Emma's chest. Unsure if the angst was derived from the thoughts of the past or present, she purposefully placed one foot in front of the other and entered the terminal's ticketing area by way of an escalator from the first to the second floor.

"Damn!" she commented under her breath stepping from the moving staircase. Slowing her pace, then stopping atop a giant silver globe—inlaid upon the terminal's large, black granite floor—a menacing spectacle caught her off guard. "Reporters!" She exhaled deeply, adjusting her grip on her suitcase.

"Well, I guess it's time for another magical McCarthy minute. You've got this," she uttered to herself, puffing out her weighty chest.

Defiantly she strolled as ladylike as possible to the North Central ticketing counter, while men sporting fedoras, with pencils and paper in hand, besieged her with questions and camera clicks. The bold, citrusy, sweet smell of Brylcreem impregnated the air as the men scurried around her, hoping to gain an exclusive interview. Emma loathed the scent, not because it stunk, but because it was the same pomade Patrick used.

"Mrs. McCarthy!" they yelled, tripping over one another physically and vocally, firing off a volley of questions. As she neared the ticketing counter, most of the reporters were now trailing her. Then suddenly, they stopped in her path. She turned to look at them.

A hush fell over the group as each anticipated a statement. Clearing her throat, then swallowing, she took a deep breath of the trendy smell of Brylcreem and licked her lips. Smartly she lowered her head and eyes in a motherly fashion, staring angrily at the boys like they had just robbed the old man's liquor cabinet.

"Boys, I have one thing to say." She held their attention as if they were about to receive top-secret information.

"The 1940s inkslinger look... it's out! As for the scent, you all bathed together in this morning... a little dab will do ya!" Emma laughed.

Standing in awe of her statement and its irrelevance to the news story they had hoped to capture, some of the men looked at one another perplexed, while others sniffed each other like little puppies catching the meaty odor of grilled steak floating on the air.

Turning her back to them, she walked the remainder of the way to the counter while most of the men retreated to the back wall. At the counter, she twisted her head around to ensure none of the men were within earshot. The flash from a photographer's camera caught her by surprise, leaving in its wake an aura of shooting stars.

She winced before saying out loud, "Damn! I hate that!"

GOLDEN GOPHER

Chapter Thirteen

———•◆•———

September 27, 1941—Seattle, Washington

The burst of light generated by the flashbulb from the reporter's camera momentarily blinded Patrick.

"So, Patrick, how does it feel to suit up for your first game in a Gopher uniform?" a reporter shot off.

"Super, just super!" he acknowledged, not sure what else to say.

"Last year you were the highest-rated prospect in the nation. Are you disappointed that you're not starting?" another chimed in.

"Coach Bierman knows who he wants on the field. Garnaas will lead the team, as he did last year. I still have a lot to learn, but if the coach wants me, I'll be ready."

"How was the trip to Seattle?" A third reporter inquired.

"L-l-l-ong!" Patrick chuckled, extending his vocalization of the word as he recalled the ride in the DC-3. The reporters laughed.

"OK, guys, that's it, eh?" Coach Bierman said, calmly

141

waving his arms back and forth, shooing the herd of reporters toward the door.

"Hey, coach, what do ya think? National Champs again?" a tall news writer hollered.

"With a little luck!" The coach replied simply in his Minnesotan accent, and with that, the men were sent on their way.

Invariably calm and collected, the Gopher leader personified the word stoic. Free from passion and unmoved by joy or grief, the gray-haired gridder turned coach provided durable guidance to his team both on and off the field.

Patrick had been highly sought after by a number of schools for his ability to run and pass the ball, but he'd said to himself, "Why go to school and play somewhere else when the best team in the nation is the home team, and the home team has a four-time national champion coach?" Plus, he knew Emma would be there.

Not known for impassioned dialogue, Bierman articulated his plan to defeat the Huskies on their home field, then sent his men out for battle. Odds were certain Patrick would have been the starting quarterback at one of the other schools that had recruited him. But he truly wanted to play for the University of Minnesota. He also knew Garnaas was in his senior year, and he wouldn't get much, if any, time on the field. Instead, he surmised that a year down the road, he'd have the job full time if he could master the playbook and demonstrate his versatility, should Bierman let him loose on the field.

The season's first contest ended in a 14-6 Golden Gopher victory. Although Patrick never took a snap, his spirited presence on the sideline solidified his leadership position among his peers.

Various legs of the Sunday flight home allowed Patrick to catch up on homework, talk with other players, and reflect on what he had learned from the bench. Arriving in Minneapolis, the team deplaned on the tarmac to a bus that took them directly to campus. A horde of students greeted the bus and cheered wildly as the men exited.

Descending the last step, Patrick wandered a few feet into the crowd, looking for Emma. That's when he felt a tap on his shoulder and turned to find her standing in front of him.

"Hi!" She almost leapt into his arms.

"Em!" A wide grin shot across his face. He dropped his bag and hugged her like he hadn't seen her in years.

"How was the trip home?"

Patrick smiled. "Exhausting, but I got some sleep on the bus ride over here." He chuckled, releasing his grip to look into her eyes.

"Well, you're home now, and you'll have plenty of time to catch up on your sleep!"

The baller laughed. "Yeah, I suppose. Hey! I have to put my gear away. Wanna wait, and when I'm done, we can take the Harley out for a ride?"

Emma stood on her tiptoes. "Sure!" She kissed him on the chin. She loved the freedom she felt riding on the back of Patrick's motorcycle. The openness, wind, speed, and vibration made her giddy. "But we can't stay out long. I have a paper I need to finish for tomorrow's class."

"No problem. I'll be back in a few, and then we'll go." Patrick looked at her dotingly.

The ride that evening felt exceptionally liberating. The cool draft created by the bike's movement through the autumn air encouraged Emma to nuzzle in close, while her long blonde hair whipped in the wind. As they approached the Minnesota River, the temperature dropped a few degrees, causing a chill to travel up her spine. Her body shivered, and her nipples became erect, prodding Patrick's back, which aroused him. He grinned, picturing her buxom chest cradled in his hands. He'd seen, touched, and held her breasts, but that was as far as he had been allowed in the year they'd been together.

As the motorcycle crossed the bridge, he removed his left hand from the handlebar and reached back to caress the side of her leg. He then stroked her knee and thigh as the bike droned over a long stretch of highway. Desiring his touch, Emma opened her leg wider, inviting his hand inside. The temptation was too intolerable, and her heart raced faster as he caressed the outside of her panties, which were now wet.

Adventurously she rubbed the bulge protruding from his khakis, clutching it one minute, then stroking it another. The distraction was too intense, the passion too unmanageable, and soon the pair found themselves parked on top of a bluff overlooking the river, where they made out.

Patrick looked at her lovingly. "Are you sure about this?" he whispered into her ear while slowly caressing her face.

"Yes!" she shot back confidently. "No reservations..."

RESERVATIONS

Chapter Fourteen

———◆———

July 19, 1968—St. Paul, Minnesota

"You must be joking!" Emma rolled her eyes.

"I'm sorry, ma'am, but there is no reservation in your name." The desk agent explained after double-checking the passenger list.

Emma laughed. "You're kidding me!"

"I'm sorry, but no, ma'am, I'm not." The portly, dark-haired girl with large brown eyes answered.

"OK, well, just sell me a ticket through to Atlanta," she huffed, slinging her purse on top of the chest-high counter.

The agent looked at her sympathetically. "I'm afraid I am unable to do that, as the flight is full."

"Again, you must be joking!" Emma responded in disbelief.

"No," the agent answered apologetically. "Our flights to your connection point in Chicago are quite popular at the moment. I can get you on the flight tomorrow morning."

"No, no, no. I need to leave today!" Emma insisted. "He

could be dead by tomorrow," she mumbled, contemplating her next move.

The agent looked at her confused. "I'm sorry, ma'am?"

"Oh, I'm sorry. My husband."

"Mrs. McCarthy, I heard about the shooting, and I'm praying for you and your family."

"Uh...ah... well, thank you, my dear. This whole thing's not your fault," Emma said, annoyed by the fact that Carrie hadn't followed through with actually purchasing the ticket.

"Can you get me a flight on another airline?" Emma sounded hopeful.

"Let me check." The agent's fingers flew over large clumsy buttons, making up the keyboard's numbers and letters.

"I am sorry, ma'am, but there is nothing else until tomorrow. All the other airlines' flights have left for the evening as well."

"Damn." She tapped the countertop with her knuckles. Placing her purse back over her arm, she scanned the terminal.

"Is there a payphone nearby?"

The agent pointed to a space over Emma's shoulder. "Yes, ma'am. Behind you on the wall to your right."

"Great," Emma thought, eyeing the newshounds still lingering in hopes of interrogating her further.

"Ah, yeah. Sorry, but the reporters over there are going to barrage me with a thousand more questions if I go that way. Are there any other phones I may use?"

"Here, ma'am," the agent said, setting a black phone connected to a long cord on top of the counter. The girl smiled empathetically. "Be my guest."

"Thank you! You're a dear!" Emma grinned, breathing a sigh of relief. Returning her purse to the counter, she adjusted the phone with her right hand, removed the handset, and placed it between her left shoulder and ear. Carefully she inserted the free index finger of her right hand into the number zero on the lower right portion of the unit's rotary dial and commenced spinning the clear plastic wheel clockwise. The phone's canny modulation brought an odd hum to her ear as she waited for an operator to pick up.

"I can help the next person in line!" The agent shouted over the echo of passengers walking and talking while transitioning the ticketing area. Skillfully the agent began assisting a curvaceous brunette who had been impatiently pacing back and forth while waiting in line behind Emma.

"Reservation name and destination?" the attendant asked.

"Cray... Barbara Cray. Atlanta," the woman replied, audibly and visibly annoyed by almost anything the agent said or did.

"Yes, ma'am, you are booked on the flight to Chicago and then on to Atlanta." The agent continued, their conversation fading into the background as a voice came over the phone line.

"Operator, how may I direct your call?" a hyper-nasal female voice inquired.

"Yes, could you get me to an operator in Atlanta, Georgia?" Emma asked.

"One moment."

A series of clicks to various switch stations along the way led to another operator.

"Operator," another nasal-infused voice, this time

with a southern drawl, answered.

"Yes, ma'am. I need the nurses' station at Georgia Baptist Hospital, please," Emma spoke as clearly as she could in her exaggerated Minnesota accent over the scratchy line. Without warning, the phone gave way to a consonant ringing.

A sturdy female voice answered, "Hello, nurses' station."

"Yes, my name is Emily McCarthy. I'm attempting to reach my daughter, Carrie, who is there with my husband, Patrick."

"OK?" The nurse replied in a doubtful tone.

Emma then added, "Is Carrie McCarthy around there by chance?"

"She may be," the woman answered skeptically.

"Listen, can you please just put her on the phone? There is a problem with my flight, and I need to speak to her."

"No offense, ma'am, but can you provide me with a description of your daughter to actually verify you are her mother."

"What? Oh, yes, she's five-foot-five with fiery-red hair, ice-blue eyes, freckles, and she can be a monumental pain in the ass when she doesn't get her way."

Convinced that the lady on the other end of the phone was who she stated, the nurse replied, "Hold on, ma'am. I'll go and get her."

The dead-accurate description and additional "monumental pain in the ass" ensured the nurse Emma was definitely her mother. No doubt Carrie had been a thorn in the nurses' asses since the moment she set foot on the ward.

Through the phone, Emma could hear the hollow sound of the phone's handset rocking to a rest on the counter as her soft shoes shuffled away, only to be replaced by the distant click of high heels characteristically worn by her daughter. A scratchy sound upset the relative calm as the phone's receiver was jostled from its resting place.

"Um, hello?" Carrie's voice clearly sounded annoyed.

"Carrie, it's Mom!"

"Mom! What's going on? You are supposed to be boarding a flight!"

"I am at the airport in Minneapolis, but there's no ticket for me!"

"Wait! What?"

"There's no ticket," Emma enunciated as clearly and loudly as she could.

"Yeah, yeah, I got it," Carrie answered, rolling her eyes. "I bought one, but the airline must have screwed it up." She lied, attempting to blame the airline for her own negligence.

Distracted by reporters hounding her for answers after she'd hung up the phone with her mother earlier that morning, Carrie had sped away from the journalists to a private waiting area, while her father underwent surgery. An hour had passed before she noticed a rotary phone sitting on a corner table, and she'd recollected the need to book a flight. Sitting lethargically, slumped in a chair, staring at the phone, she had weighed the financial cost of an airline ticket and had ultimately decided her money would be better spent elsewhere.

"What's the worst that can happen?" she had thought. "She gets there and has to buy the ticket herself." Carrie then had crossed her arms and reclined further into the seat by placing her feet up on a chair that she'd pulled in front of her.

"That's the least she can do." Carrie had smiled fiendishly, a gleam of satisfaction twinkled in her eye as though she were "sticking it to her mother" by requiring Emma to purchase her own ticket.

"So buy one!" Carrie shot back angrily.

"I can't! The flight's full, and the earliest I can fly out is tomorrow morning," Emma sternly returned.

"Well, I don't know what you want me to do!" Carrie's snotty adolescent rebuttal crackled through the receiver. She'd never considered a scenario in which her mother wouldn't be able to obtain a ticket due to a full or overbooked flight.

"Did you check with the other airlines? Don't they have a flight you can get on?" she asked, trying to consider other possibilities and now worried her father may pay the price for her negligence.

"Yes," Emma grumbled.

"Well, then just get here as soon as you can. Take the flight out tomorrow morning if that's all that's available."

Emma didn't want to ask, fearing another childish comment, but did. "How's your father?"

"He's in surgery. I don't know; I'm not a doctor like you."

"OK, well I just wanted you to know what's happening and that whomever you told to get the ticket never followed through."

Carrie released a heavy huff on the other end, knowing that she was the only one to blame. "Yeah, OK. Just get here as soon as you can!"

"I will. And Carrie ... I love—" A harsh click cut off Emma's sentence, followed by a dial tone.

"You," Emma still finished her sentence even though Carrie had hung up. As she placed the receiver back into its base, she felt disbelief.

Cradling the phone between her thumb and index fingers, Emma used her pinky finger to press the hang-up lever, ending the call. Instantly she considered her options, when an old friend came to mind.

"Excuse me, miss. May I make another call?" she asked the agent.

"Of course, Mrs. McCarthy."

FRIENDS IN HIGH PLACES

Chapter Fifteen

———◆———

July 19, 1968—Minneapolis
St. Paul International Airport

Emma placed her handbag next to the phone on the counter and pulled out a small address book. Flopping it down next to the phone, Emma thumbed through the first couple of pages, frantically looking for a phone number.

"Adams, Ahrens, Albert... I know too many frickin' people whose last names begin with the letter a!" she growled. "Andersson! There it is!" She pressed her index finger to the page, just below the name, and then began spinning the phone's rotary dial. After a quick couple of rings, she heard a man's deep, confident voice. "Hello."

"Hello... Cal, is that you?"

"Yes, this is Calvin."

"Cal, it's Emma. How are you?" she asked, her voice still slightly agitated from the last call.

"Hey, Em! Sorry I didn't immediately recognize your voice, it's been a while. How are you?"

"Well, I'm at the airport, trying to get to Atlanta. Something happened to Patrick, and I can't get a commercial flight out until tomorrow."

With a concerned tone, Cal said, "Yeah, I heard. I'm sorry. Is there anything I can do?"

"That's kind of why I'm calling. I know you used to have a plane. Do you still own one?"

"Yeah, yeah! I'm half owner of a small plane that's based at Fleming Field."

"I know this is a huge inconvenience, but is there any way you would be able to fly me to Atlanta? Carrie demanded I fly down in case Patrick doesn't make it." Her voice sounded even more irritated now instead of distressed, as thoughts of her daughter's insolent words crossed her mind.

Emma could hear what sounded like pages being shuffled around before Cal responded, "Gee, Em, I'd love to, but I'm booked with patients. Hey, I tell you what. I can phone Tom Mulvaney; he's the guy I'm part owner with of the plane. He's an old navy fighter pilot. I'm sure he'd love a good cross-country flight."

"Would you check, Cal? I'm just about out of options unless I want to purchase a ticket and wait until tomorrow. I can reimburse you for the time and fuel."

"That's not necessary. What number can I call you back at?"

"Miss," Emma momentarily moved the lower portion of the handset away from her mouth. "What's the number here?"

"612-726-5555," the young lady replied.

"Sorry. Can you just say the numbers slowly as I repeat them on the phone so that I'm sure I have the right number?"

153

"Yes ma'am." The agent slowly began again, as Emma repeated the numbers to Cal.

"OK. Give me a few minutes, and I'll call you back."

"Thanks!" Emma returned the receiver to its base.

A few minutes later, the ticketing agent answered the phone and then handed it to Emma.

"All right. Tom can meet you at Fleming Field in an hour and a half. Do you remember where that is?"

Emma thought for a second. "Yes, South Saint Paul."

"Correct. When you get there, look for a single-engine Piper Comanche. It's a low wing, white with blue-and-red pinstripes. Do you know what I mean by a low wing?"

"Sure, you took me up in it once."

"Oh, that's right! Anyway, Tom should have it pre-flighted and gassed up by the time you get there. Just park in the grass behind the plane, and Tom will grab your bags."

"OK. Thank you so much, Cal!"

Cal stated in an affectionate tone, "Anything for you, Em. Hang in there, and call me when you can."

"I will. Goodbye!" Emma placed the receiver back into its cradle.

The agent looked at Emma. "I assume you don't need me to book you on tomorrow morning's flight?"

"No, but thank you. I have a friend who can fly me."

"It's always good to have friends in high places." The friendly agent giggled.

"It certainly is." Emma thanked the girl again before covertly making her way past the reporters huddled by the back wall and sneaking out of the terminal.

Perplexed by Emma's sudden disappearance, two of the fellows wearing fedoras approached the counter. The sweet, but overpowering scent of Brylcreem overtook the desk agent, causing the young woman's nostrils to flare as she debated whether or not she should engage the men in conversation. She attempted to ignore them, but one of the reporters obnoxiously cleared his throat which summoned her attention.

"Excuse me, miss?"

"Yes?"

"The lady who was just here, do you know where she went?" A thick midwestern accent spilled from his mouth.

"Who, the brunette woman?" She acted inane. "She should be at the gate boarding her flight."

"No, no, the blonde who was standing here just a minute ago, using the phone."

Buying time for Emma, she drew out the conversation. "Oh, the blonde-haired lady. What about her?"

"Yeah, that one. Do you know where she went?"

"Oh, she mentioned forgetting something in her car. She'll be right back," the young lady fibbed, convincing the men Emma would return momentarily before returning her attention to assisting other patrons.

INDULGENCE

Chapter Sixteen

July 19, 1968—Mendota Heights, Minnesota

It was 7:00 p.m. by the time Emma departed the terminal for Fleming Field. The sun had begun its descent toward the west, so there was a cool breeze. The sun's hue and warmth radiated a sensual and seductive ambiance, indicative of the first time Emma and Patrick had made love.

As Emma drove over the Mendota Bridge, her mind relived the evening she and Patrick had taken his Harley out for a ride and stopped at a secluded tourist observation point, off Highway 13, a few short miles south of the bridge. Not much had changed along the route, even the weather conditions had begun to mimic that autumn evening.

"It was perfect," she recalled with a grin. A victorious homecoming had created a euphoric frenzy that culminated in the surrender of her virginity atop Patrick's 1937 Harley-Davidson Knucklehead.

As she approached the end of the bridge, a stoplight

that had been set in place to direct traffic gave Emma enough time to glance at her watch. "A diversion to the overlook wouldn't take long," she said to herself, seriously considering the idea before turning the Bonneville's steering wheel to the right and proceeding down the road to the observation point. Within minutes, the vehicle was parked at the end of a round gravel lot overlooking the Minnesota River in the exact spot the motorcycle had been parked twenty-seven years earlier.

Without pause, Emma allowed herself to indulge in the serene setting as the memory of what had happened between her and Patrick so many years prior washed over her. Looking at the bluffs on the other side of the river, she alternated her attention between an old military fort towering over the junction of the Mississippi and Minnesota rivers to the right and structures of Minneapolis-St. Paul International Airport to the left.

The area hadn't changed much. Large, lengthy logs laying on their sides still marked the boundaries of the observation point. Ducks and geese flew low and unaffected over the water as airplanes made their way above them toward the airport. Long blades of grass and weeds slightly obscured portions of the view and timelessly fluttered in the wind as they speckled steep, sandy bluffs, which sheltered creatures from humans and predators. Yet it was also different.

Time had changed some aspects of the lookout. A historical marker now sat where there hadn't been one before. Jet engines replaced propellers, drowning out nature's songs as the planes made their approach. And the young woman she had been back in the day was no longer young.

Sitting silently in her convertible, she still held the wheel while her eyes scanned the landscape straight ahead. But in her mind, her eyes were actually moving from Patrick's large, round, loving eyes to the squareness of his determined jaw and the image of his hand rising affectionately to touch her cheek. Gently he held her face in his strong hands, caressing her lips with the tip of his thumb. The warmth of his touch conveyed his adoration, while his nose brushed over hers, nuzzling it softly.

Tilting his head, Patrick kissed Emma slowly, running his hands over the sides of her face and through her long hair. Sliding his palm down her spine to the small of her back, he drew Emma closer and kissed her tenderly. She could feel the warmth of his breath against her ear as he whispered, "I love you so much."

Emma was surprised by how her memory could still generate such a longing for him. She missed the simplicity of their lives, and her body ached for the way only he could make her feel.

Enthralled by a combination of place and reflection, Emma was thrown into the intensity of the moment, as she slid down deeper into the seat. Her thoughts returned to the Harley. Patrick had gently laid her back against the motorcycle's gas tank. Remembering their lovemaking, she unbuttoned the lower portion of her blouse. In her mind, her hands became his, while she slowly ran her fingertips over her navel to her breasts, like he had done all those years ago. With the other hand, she mimicked his touch, caressing the outside of her thigh. Gliding considerably lower into the seat only aided in her skirt hiking up, as it had that day against the motorcycle's tank.

Opening her blouse and exposing her breasts, Emma

could feel the smile spreading on her face as she envisioned Patrick holding and caressing them. Recollection of his lips softly kissing hers while his fingers slid slowly down to the unkempt rise of curly red hair awakened something deep within her.

Sliding her hand from the outside of her thigh to her center, she alternated the intensity of her touch as he had—massaging her lightly, then firmly, while he explored her moistening skin, which only magnified her desire. Running her hand across her breasts, down her waist, and back up, she caressed her firming nipples. Rhythmically, her fingers on the other hand circled just under the fine hair, slipping inside and back out.

Easing her legs further apart, she could remember feeling him enter her, sending a rush of heat through her body. The image and fullness of him inside her increased the cadenced stroking. Firmly she advanced and withdrew her fingers as she recalled the fulfilling pleasure he had given her. Each advance recreated the indulgence of his strong body moving against hers—the two interwoven as they became one. Emma couldn't resist the building waves of pure satisfaction, which were a result from the memory. Quivering uncontrollably, she drew her legs together, trapping her hand, as she remembered how she had held him in place. Heat had risen from their bodies, producing intense tremors. Reaching her climax, she gasped for air and vividly embraced him. Afterward, she relaxed her body, smiling contently and expecting to find him staring lovingly back at her after opening her eyes. But in place of his admiration, the sun's setting glare off the car's windshield was all that greeted her. And the sky's colors forming on the horizon disoriented her.

Confused, Emma's eyes scanned the bluff on the other side of the river in an attempt to resolve her mind's deception. Frantically she checked her surroundings, replacing the blouse over her exposed breasts. Dropping her hands to her hips, she repositioned herself in the seat, inching her skirt back into place. Tears welled in her eyes, then flowed down her cheeks as a plethora of emotions overwhelmed her. No matter how hard she tried to forget, or how much she wanted to hate, she couldn't let go of Patrick, her first love. She choked back the sobs that threatened to consume her. Looking into the rearview mirror, she reminded herself of the promise she'd made never to look back. But no matter which way she moved the mirror, her longing for him was always there, stalking her.

Sighing heavily and wiping away the tears, she recast herself to look as proper as possible before returning upright in the seat. Anxiously she repositioned herself and scrutinized her look.

"I may be forty-five, but I still got it." She proudly grinned, pushing stray strands of hair away from her view. Reaching into her purse, she retrieved a small canister of lipstick, popped the top, and rotated the bottom, drawing the pigmented wax up through the opening. Effortlessly she applied the rich color to her lips, then withdrew it, blowing a smooch in the air. "Take that, Marilyn!" Emma giggled as she compared herself to the buxom actress.

Returning the lipstick to her bag, she adjusted herself for the drive. Within seconds, she reclaimed the puritanical role of a political spouse and physician. Noticing a vehicle turning into the observation point from the road, Emma took a deep breath and exhaled, her heart still racing from the self-gratifying experience. Rotating the square ignition key, the Bonneville's engine turned over without a hitch. Shifting the car into drive, she idled the vehicle forward a few feet, then accelerated, slightly freeing the wheel to spin easier. Cutting sharply to the right to avoid the oncoming vehicle, she let it pass, then drove the Bonneville toward the exit. As she advanced, she subconsciously noticed the passing vehicle contained a couple of teenagers—undoubtedly looking for their own spot to park. Parking in the place where Emma had just departed, they became so wrapped up in their own passion that they barely noticed the Bonneville leaving the area.

"Ah, young love," Emma thought, speeding away.

THE FLIGHT

Chapter Seventeen

——————

July 19, 1968—South St. Paul, Minnesota

Overlooking the Mississippi River, Fleming Field buzzed with activity as small aircraft navigated the airspace overhead. The sound of propeller blades splitting the wind intensified and then diminished, as the engines that powered them surged, lifting the winged cages skyward before disappearing into the distance. The sun had dipped below the horizon. Emma maneuvered the Bonneville through a fence opening that provided access to the aircraft apron and grass tie-down area. Fumes from a set of nearby pumps dispensing aviation gas into private airplanes dawdled in the air. A light west wind carried the vapor across the field, causing the airfield's windsock to fluctuate back and forth.

A tall, slender fellow dressed in a timeworn leather flight jacket walked intently around the aircraft, probing for damage or issues that would make the plane unairworthy. The slight push of one control surface made the opposing surface move, signifying their linkage.

Searching meticulously for dents, cracks, creases, missing cotter keys, screws, bolts, or pins, the man bent down and crawled his way around the plane, looking for any discrepancies. A check of the engine and its oil level satisfied the dark-haired man, who was styling a '50s crew cut, pair of aviator sunglasses, and khaki trousers. When he saw Emma arrive, he decided to forego the rest of his evaluation so that he could assist Emma from her vehicle, which was now parked directly behind the plane's tail.

"Oh, thank you," Emma stated tired and overwhelmed as he offered his hand, helping her out of the car.

"Hello, Dr. McCarthy. My name is Tom Mulvaney, but please, call me Tom."

"Well, it's very nice to meet you, Tom." She sighed heavily. "Please call me Emma," She smiled.

"Is everything ok?" Tom inquired concerned by the look on her face and the haggard breath.

"Oh, yes, yes. It's just been a very trying day." She nodded, catching the light, effervescent scent of Brylcreem drifting from his head.

Flaring her nostrils, she asked, "Brylcreem, eh?"

"I'm sorry?" Tom replied, unsure of what she had asked.

"Your hair"—her hand swirled around the top of her head— "let me guess ... Brylcreem?"

"Oh yeah!" He laughed proudly. "Just a dab will do ya! Right, Doc?" He happily recited the product's tagline.

"Ah ... yeah," Emma uttered, smiling sarcastically. "By the way, please don't call me Doc. Just Emma."

"Very nice to meet you ... just Emma." He half-smiled after seeing her expression that screamed she wasn't amused by his comment.

"Did you bring a suitcase?" Tom asked, looking at the car.

"Oh yes. I placed it in the back seat."

After swiftly departing the commercial airport's terminal, Emma determined it would be easier to toss the bag in the back seat versus going through the whole rigmarole of finding the key, opening the trunk, stowing the bag, closing the trunk, and then climbing into the car. She had been in such a hurry to avoid the reporters that she hadn't even bothered to retract the convertible's top.

"Hey, Doc?" Tom began, only to receive a look from Emma that signaled displeasure with his word selection. "Sorry ... Emma. Do you have a coat or sweater with you?"

"Yes. There's one in my suitcase."

"You may want to put it on before we get airborne. With the sun setting, it's going to get quite chilly once we get aloft."

Fetching the suitcase from the back seat, Tom gently placed it on the hood, providing easy access to the bag. Quickly, Emma popped it open, removed the sweater, draped it over her shoulders, then shut and latched the suitcase. It wasn't until she had placed the sweater over her shoulders that she realized how chilly it had become. As she followed Tom to the plane, a poignant whiff of aviation gas recaptured a period of uneasiness and angst in her life, which she had long since consigned to oblivion.

Placing her bag on the ground, just in front of the leading edge of the wing on the passenger side of the airplane, Tom faced the wing, stabilized himself, and kicked away a lone wooden set of chocks blocking the landing gear. One had been placed in the front and back of each wheel to ensure the craft didn't roll anywhere, which was a customary practice to ensure the brakes were released after the plane was parked and the engine shut down.

Emma stood patiently off the wing tip and watched as the flier picked her bag off the ground and proceeded from the front of the wing. Around the wingtip and then to the trailing edge, he walked, arriving at the side of the plane's fuselage, where he popped open a small baggage compartment and placed the bag on its back before strapping it to the floor. Closing the cargo door, he stepped lightly onto the top of the wing, traversing a painted area on the passenger side of the craft, where the wing root and fuselage joined. Opening the only door to the cabin, the pilot climbed into the space and situated himself in the pilot's seat.

After summoning Emma to the compartment, Tom began to prepare the aircraft for engine start. Emma made her way to the plane's side. With her purse in hand, she steadied herself, first climbing on top of the wing, then carefully navigating the walkway in heels. Hunching, she lowered herself feet first into the craft, closed the door, adjusted the small, white vinyl seat, and settled in for the flight. The sky was growing darker by the moment, and an annoying high-pitched whine in the cabin droned on like tinnitus, ringing endlessly in her ears. In front of her, the airplane's instrument panel was lit by a faint white light that was strategically positioned in the top center of the plane's glare shield. The instruments' backlighting glowed various colors of red and amber, drawing her attention to the assorted communication and navigation devices.

"Clear!" Tom's loud and sudden announcement startled Emma. But then she was further surprised by the abrupt rotation of the propeller and the burst of power from the 180 horse, four-cylinder Lycoming engine, which was jostling the craft from side to side in the prop's wake. In front of her, the yoke rolled left and right, then moved forward and aft. Tom checked for freedom of movement in the ailerons and elevator. Emma had rested her feet on two large pedals that were dangling from a torque tube assembly in front of the firewall below, when she realized her heels needed to be removed if she planned on attaining any level of comfort during the flight. Slipping them off and shoving them back toward the seat, she repositioned her bare feet back on the pedals, which moved independently of one another, while Tom performed the same freedom of movement checks on the rudder.

Reaching over from the pilot's seat, Tom handed her a headset, then placed one on his head. Using both hands to spread the earpieces apart, Emma slipped it over her head and ears. The padded ear seals that were attached to the band dulled the noise engulfing the cabin, as a tone alternating in intensity could be heard in the background.

"Can you hear me?" Tom asked, looking over at her.

Emma nodded.

"Just push the button on the yoke to talk. Press the top portion of the rocker switch to talk to me, and the bottom to talk to folks outside the plane." He said, providing a quick lesson.

"Yep, I've got it!" her voice shot over the intercom.

"Good! OK, let's get this show on the road!"

Prior to engine start, Tom had set the brakes of the craft so that it wouldn't roll. Releasing the brakes and freeing the wheels allowed the plane to move forward a few feet before he reapplied them momentarily to verify they were working as they should.

"Ah yes," she recalled as the craft began rolling, "I remember this!" Her mind drifted back in time, remembering a portion of her life from when she'd lived in south-central Kansas.

Wichita, Kansas was a long way from St. Paul, Minnesota, but that's where her mind sauntered off to as the plane taxied to a run-up area, which was close to the hold short line at the end of the runway. Steering the plane into the wind, stopping, and then setting the brakes, Tom throttled up the engine and tested its performance before takeoff. In the minutes it took to complete the check, Emma thought about Patrick's obsession with becoming a pilot—and how a surprise attack changed their lives, leading them in a direction neither had anticipated.

RECRUITS

Chapter Eighteen

December 8, 1941—U of M Student Union

"Yesterday, December 7, 1941—a date that will live in infamy—the United States of America was suddenly and deliberately attacked by naval and air forces of the Empire of Japan!"

An old Zenith radio crackled, echoing off the granite floor and walls of the student union, as the distinctive voice of President Roosevelt trumpeted over the airwaves. Patrick, Emma, and a group of friends stood silently around the small, wooden radio that emitted the musty, humid scent of the root cellar it had obviously been rescued from. The stench now filled the nostrils of anyone within a few feet of its position. Listening in disbelief, the students anxiously hung on every word the president said as he made a case for going to war with the Empire of Japan.

Breaking free from the assembly, Patrick and a number of other young men began a determined discussion on the other side of the union. Suddenly noticing him absent from her side, Emma wandered the hall and searched for Patrick. Locating him on the other side of the room, she saw he was engaged in conversation. Moving in behind him, Emma stopped momentarily to listen to the discussion. The men were animated in their talk of enlisting and fighting the Japanese. It took a firm touch on his back and tug of his shirt to gain Patrick's attention. Still engaged in conversation with the group, he turned to find Emma standing behind him. His face held an expression she hadn't seen before. A conglomeration of hate, fear, determination, and courage lit up his complexion. Before she could even speak, he revealed his desire to fight.

"I feel like I need to join up, Em!" Patrick declared. He had been clearly stirred to action by the bombing and the president's speech.

"Wait ... what? What about school? I know you want to go, but they haven't even made a call yet for men to go fight!" Emma challenged, attempting to get him to consider what he was saying.

"What do you mean? The draft has been going on since September of last year. I spoke with Jack this morning on the phone. He and Bob Olsen want me to come home, so we can all enlist together."

Standing there in awe, Emma attempted to apprehend the words circling in her head—words that she wanted to convey to him. "Wait. This is crazy! You just need to slow down and see what happens first."

"I want to fly, Em. If I sign up now, I have a better chance of getting a pilot slot than if I get drafted. If that happens, I'll probably end up in the infantry."

"OK, but what about Jack and Bob? Do they want to be pilots as well? Is it really going to matter if you enlist tomorrow or a month from now? You guys may not even end up fighting in the same unit!" Emma exclaimed, throwing her hands in the air.

"Em, I need to do this. I'm leaving for Bemidji in the morning. I'd really like you to come with me?"

"I can't just walk away from school—and neither should you! You need to be reasonable about this and—"

"Be reasonable? Em! We are at war! If we don't sign up and fight, we may not have a school to come back to!" He scowled as his body stiffened and he clenched his fists.

Afraid, Emma cowered slightly. It was the first time in the year they'd been together that she had witnessed such outrage from him. Speechless, she stood small in front of him as other students, who were within earshot of the argument, timidly looked on.

"If you don't want to leave school, fine." He lowered his voice a bit after observing the other students staring at him. "But I cannot sit here"—he pointed at the floor—"and pretend everything is hunky-dory, while Jack and Bob go off and fight!"

Relaxing his grip and intensity, he continued, "Let me know what you want to do. I love you, but I'm leaving at 10:00 a.m." he announced without wavering, then walked off, leaving her dumbfounded and in a puddle of tears.

Wiping her eyes, Emma noticed a figure approach her and offer what appeared to be a white cloth. "Are you OK?" a deep, intelligent voice inquired.

"Yes." Still sniffling, she used the man's handkerchief to dry her eyes. The scent from the linen gave off a familiar aroma, which she recognized from class.

"Oh ... Cal. It's you," she said, blinking, now able to identify who was assisting her.

"Yeah! Hi, Emma." He put on a half-grin, holding his hands at the ready to offer aid. Calvin Andersson knew Emma from the human structure and function class they shared. Six feet tall and roughly 210 pounds, his head held a gratuitous amount of lush, dark hair that complemented an astonishing handsomeness and a fit physique. His fair complexion screamed Swedish-Minnesotan, and if that wasn't enough to satisfy a guess at his heritage, Cal's love for lutefisk was a dead giveaway.

He asked with concern in his voice, "Is there anything I can help you with?"

"No," she reassured. "It's just that my boyfriend wants to enlist."

"Well, to be honest, I was considering doing the same thing. I want to do something to help in the medical field, though I doubt I will be able to do much other than be a medic." He sounded disappointed at the prospect.

"You would be good at that. But I'd rather not see any of you guys go."

Emma's compliment and concern reminded him of his mother. Cal was positive she would probably give him the same response.

"Someone's gotta go, Emma. It's just what we have to do. No one wants to go, but what happens if we don't? Personally, I'd rather die than live under the rule of the Nazis or Japs!" His sincere dialogue sensibly argued his point.

Emma agreed, nodding reluctantly.

"Hey." Cal touched her arm lightly. "Come on. This could be the last time I see you. If we part ways and you don't have that perfect smile on your face that I've seen you wearing every day since the beginning of school, it's going to ruin my whole war," he joked.

Emma laughed, wiping the last of her tears away.

"Here." She held up his handkerchief, which was now damp with her tears. "You may need this." Emma presented it to him like an award.

"Oh yeah. Can't forget that." He retrieved it from her grip and placed it in his pants pocket. "Hey, I'll see you back here after we kick Hirohito's ass, OK?" He made an attempt to lighten the mood.

"OK," Emma laughed, nodding her head again.

"Bye, Emma!" Cal waved as he backed away.

Emma watched while her friend disappeared into the crowd. Suddenly she recalled the argument she'd had with Patrick. Making her way from the union to her dorm room, she snatched two suitcases from the closet and began pulling clothes from her dresser. Unsure if she would return, she attempted to pack as many items as she could into the suitcases. Unable to fit everything, she called her grandparents to inform them of her plan, then asked if they would drop by later and move the rest of the items to their house until she could return to St. Paul.

Lying in bed that night, she was too conflicted to sleep. She had ensured that before the end of the quarter, her grandparents would remove from her room whatever belongings she hadn't taken. But she still hadn't convinced herself to leave. She mulled over staying at school, concluding that if Patrick was going to enlist and go to war, he wouldn't be around anyway. So worrying about him whether she was in Bemidji or St. Paul really didn't make a difference. Then she convinced herself remaining in St. Paul would be selfish. Still, the decision weighed heavily on her conscience as the sun broke through the clouds the next morning. But she knew if she didn't go with him and something happened to him, she would regret it for the rest of her life.

The next morning was difficult for her. After donning her favorite light blue trench coat, which extended to her knees, and blue Gaytees campus boots, she mourned her departure as she shut off the light and closed the door to the room. Shuffling swiftly down the corridor, Emma could feel her soul hurting and her heart pounding as her bags banged between her legs and the thick brick walls of the hall. Exiting the building, she made her way to a nearby parking lot where Patrick kept the 1934 Chrysler Airflow, which his father had purchased for him their last year of high school. She placed the suitcases she'd packed on the pavement, near the vehicle's bustle-back trunk, and then she settled her derriere on top of the larger of the two. Crossing her arms and legs, she huddled over them in an attempt to keep herself warm while patiently waiting for Patrick to show.

Emma had arrived at the car around 9:50 a.m. and had sat in the frigid Minnesota cold for another twelve minutes before Patrick finally arrived, seated in the passenger seat of a teammate's car. Exiting the vehicle, he turned quickly toward the back seat of his buddy's car and wrestled a large duffle bag from within. Wishing the driver good luck, he slammed the door shut and turned toward Emma.

"I see you decided to go." Patrick smartly eyed her.

Looking up, she hissed, "Any decent fellow would have stopped by and assisted me with my bags! Furthermore, you stated 10:00 a.m.! It's 10:02!" Emma huffed angrily, her breath trailing off into a wispy white cloud as she lifted her sleeve to peer at her watch.

"I wasn't sure if you were coming with me." He tossed the duffle over his shoulder and placed his hands in the pockets of his letterman jacket.

"You never asked," she countered, shivering in the bitter cold while peering off into the distance.

"I'm sorry," he said, attempting to appease her, though she could see the hollowness of his apology. "Can we just go? I want to get on the road. The sun's setting earlier and earlier." He changed the subject, looking toward the sky.

"Yeah?" She projected a badgered look of disbelief from her perch. Pissed off, she remained impervious to his apology as she paraded to the passenger side of Patrick's streamlined sedan. Impatiently she stood, waiting for him to open the door. Catching her hint, he followed, gripping the handle and engaging the door's release with his thumb, allowing it to swing open. After Emma climbed in, he shut the door, then proceeded to the trunk, opening a sloping rear body panel and stowing the luggage.

Moving to the driver's side, he got in, situated himself, and then exhaled loudly. Glancing at the back of Emma's head as she stared out the passenger window, he knew idle conversation would be like poking a wounded grizzly bear, so he decided to forego making a comment.

After Patrick placed the key in the ignition, the straight-eight engine roared to a start. He engaged the transmission and pulled from the parking lot, beginning the seven-hour journey to Bemidji.

The days and weeks that followed their return home were filled with uncertainty, as the United States collectively caught its breath after the sucker punch it had received on December 7th. Christmas came and went, while the nation mobilized its resources and began turning

174

out armaments and machinery to combat their enemies in Europe and Asia.

Men, young and old, flocked to military induction centers where they were given physical and psychological examinations. Patrick McCarthy, Jack Johnson, and Bob Olsen were just three of thousands overrunning the centers to start the induction process.

After starting classes at the university, Emma had telephoned home on a number of occasions to speak with her father. She recalled how tired he would be after working extremely long hours, evaluating young men for duty after Congress had approved the first peacetime draft in September of 1940. The doctors were now even more overworked, as they hurried through exams to get men into the fight.

The attack on Pearl Harbor by the Japanese was personal. The United States could not isolate itself from war any longer. Emma and Patrick waited patiently for news from the local draft board. They were at Patrick's parents one afternoon, when his draft letter arrived from the war department ...

IV-F

Chapter Nineteen

July 19, 1968–Cherokee 1868K

Pilot: "Minneapolis Center, Cherokee 1868 Kilo."

Air Traffic Control (ATC): "Cherokee 1868K, go ahead."

Pilot: "Good evening. Cherokee 68K, just departed South St Paul Fleming field, at 2,000 feet climbing to 9,500, requesting VFR flight following to Bardstown, BRY (Bravo, Romeo, Yankee)."

ATC: "Cherokee 68K, Squawk 4323 and identify.

Pilot: "Squawk 4323 and identify."

Tom turned a knob on the plane's identification and flight following feature, then pushed a small black button, allowing the air traffic controller on the ground to locate the plane on his radar scope.

ATC: Cherokee 86K, radar contact, cleared to enter Class Bravo airspace, fly heading 167, climb and maintain 9,500, maintain VFR. Flight plan activated at 0235 Zulu, Minneapolis altimeter 29.92. We'd appreciate any pilot reports on Flight Watch, 122.0."

Pilot: Cleared to enter Class Bravo airspace, fly heading 167, ascend climb and maintain 9,500, maintain VFR, Cherokee 86K.

"How are you doing, Emma?" Tom's commanding voice interrupted her thoughts.

"I'm fine, just fine. Thanks for recommending the sweater. I forgot how chilly it can be once you get up here." She crossed her arms, pulling the ends of the sweater closer together to retain body heat.

"If you'd like, we can turn up the heat a little." Tom noted the aircraft heating control regulator in front of her, on the far right side of the instrument panel.

"Where?" Emma searched the panel, which was obscured by the lack of light and the plane's yoke that had moved slightly in front of her to make small adjustments to the aircraft's altitude while it climbed to cruising altitude.

"If you look at the very top right side of the panel, there's a round gauge. Just follow it straight down, and there are two levers. I can't remember which one, but one of those controls the amount of heat we get in the cabin. "Have you flown before?" Tom watched as she slid the knobs, independently controlling the temperature and flow.

She smiled and asked, "You mean other than on the airlines? Yes. My husband used to fly a lot. We lived in Kansas during the war, and he used to be in an aero club. On occasion, he would take me up with him to build flight hours. He hoped the army would eventually grant him a waiver to fly in the air corps but they never did."

Arriving at cruising altitude, Tom leveled off the aircraft and throttled back the engine. The sky had grown dark, and lights of various colors and intensity flickered off the landscape below.

Interested, Tom asked, "What did he need a waiver for?"

"Hiatal hernia," she remarked.

"What? He was deferred for a hernia?" He asked, clearly flabbergasted. That's like a deferment for an ingrown toenail!" Tom chortled and shook his head, inwardly burning Patrick in effigy.

"Yeah, he was surprised, too, and vocally conveyed his displeasure after the IV-F rating letter from the war department was delivered. He just didn't do it as eloquently. I'm sure it was a difficult time for him though. He had been the nation's most sought-after high school football recruit, rode the Gopher bench his whole freshman year as a second-stringer, and hoped to take the reins as starting QB in '42. So when the war broke out—"

"Wait! Your husband played football at the U of M?" Tom's eyes widened in the faint light as he turned toward her, clearly jarred by the information.

"Yes." Tapping her foot on the floor, Emma felt anxious but then realized she was really feeling anger brewing within at Tom's hernia comment. She caught herself subconsciously defending the one man in the world who enraged her the most.

"Uh-ha." Tom returned his gaze to the instrument panel, searching twenty-seven years into the recesses of his mind for the names of the players he could remember from the '41 Minnesota Golden Gopher football team. The only one he could recall was Bruce "Bob" Smith, who had run away with the Heisman that year.

"As I was going to say, so when war broke out and

President Roosevelt made an impassioned speech to Congress, calling for war, I'm sure the disappointment Patrick felt from riding the bench all season was lost on the premise he would definitely play first string on the field of battle. He believed delivering bombs via aircraft to the enemy was of greater importance than delivering a football from his arm to a receiver in the end zone."

Looking at the instrument panel, Tom couldn't remember any of the other players' names, save one. "What's your husband's name?"

"You mean Cal didn't tell you?" Emma looked at him, believing it was strange that Cal hadn't told Tom why he was flying to Atlanta.

"Tell me what? He said he had a 'doctor friend' who desperately needed to get to Atlanta and asked if I was up for a long cross-country," the aviator replied.

"You don't follow the news or politics much, do you, Tom?" Emma chuckled, still reeling a little from his comment earlier about Patrick's IV-F rating.

"News, sometimes. Politics and politicians ... no. Politicians got us into Korea and Vietnam, and I prefer to avoid shit that gets young men shot and killed." He doggedly defended against her snooty remark, as a red glow from the plane's instruments lit up the whites of his eyes.

"Touché," Emma said. "So, 'my husband'"—she made quotes in the air with her fingers— "is Patrick McCarthy, Senator Eugene McCarthy's cousin and chief of staff."

Perplexed, Tom asked, "You mean the guys who were shot yesterday?"

"Yup." Emma half nodded. Discombobulated, she retracted her gaze from Tom and shifted it toward the instrument panel in front of her. At first, she blamed the turbulent kinetics involved with the aircraft moving through the atmosphere as the reason why she felt odd, but looking out the window at the lights covering the earth below, she knew that wasn't the case at all. Emma reflected on the man she knew and loved in high school and college. Then she thought about the man she'd grown to hate. After years of separation and bitterness, she was conflicted about her feelings for him. "How can I still love him so deeply yet continue to hate him so intensely?" she wondered privately.

Tom didn't immediately respond to the information Emma had offered, since he was still irritated by what he perceived as sarcasm. Silence fell over the cabin, as the drone of the plane's propeller hummed on. Through the headset anchored over her ears, idle chatter of distant pilots communicating with air traffic control crackled beneath the hum of the propeller, like scratchy old records. Through a vent over the glare shield, warm air diffused into the cabin, picking up a hint of new car smell from recently refurbished vinyl seats. The scent blew into Emma's nostrils. The cold air outside the craft chilled the window, where she rested her shoulder, as it attempted to penetrate the heated compartment.

Without warning, the intercom clicked. "So, how is it a highly recruited high school quarterback on a championship college team ends up in politics and not playing in the National Football League?" Tom asked, looking at her as though he already had the answer. "The war?"

"No," Emma quickly conveyed, clicking the talk portion of the intercom's rocker switch while shaking her head slowly and focusing on his gaze. The buzz of electrical current bustling over the headset's speakers increased with the release of the rocker switch, then died as she clicked it again to speak.

"Rucker!" Her somber voice matched the devastated expression on her face...

HINES

Chapter Twenty

———◆———

July 19, 1968—Somewhere over Illinois

Some time had passed before Tom and Emma spoke again. Tom wasn't sure what to make of her "Rucker" comment, or how it led her husband into politics versus the NFL.

After leveling off at 9,500 feet, Tom had set the craft to cruise at 140 knots, which it had done for a little over an hour, when a glowing city off the pilot's side of the plane approached below. Convinced the reason behind her husband's detour into politics was none of his concern, Tom decided he'd keep to himself and do what he had volunteered to do—fly the plane. The uneasy silence was broken a little later when Emma noticed a large luminous area below.

"Tom, what city is that?"

Glancing at the chart lying on his lap, then peering out the window to verify, he answered, "We are near DeKalb, Illinois. So that glowing menagerie over there should be the shithole they call Chicago."

"You don't like Chicago?" Emma questioned, gazing at

the beauty of a million city lights lining the streets and illuminating the sky.

"I'm not very fond of the place, no. There's one spot in particular I really hate, and it sits on the west side." Tom stiffened his neck, pointing toward an area at about the ten o'clock position, off the plane's nose.

Emma laughed. "Let me guess. Hines Veterans Hospital."

"You know the joint?"

"Ah, all too well." Emma scowled. "How did you end up there?"

An extended period of silence drew her attention to Tom and his blank stare. He released the tension from his neck, settled uneasily into his seat, and rotated the trim wheel back to add a little extra pressure on the elevator so that the nose of the plane would come up slightly. A heavy sigh proceeded the familiar sound of the aircraft's intercom system engaging, then disengaging. Emma could sense the subject was something extremely difficult for him to discuss, and she broke in before he could press the button again.

"I mean, if you don't want to tell me, that's fine. It's really none of my business!" she adamantly declared, releasing the switch.

A click ensued. "I flew the F4 Corsair in World War II, the F9 Panther in Korea, and two stints in Vietnam, flying the F-4 Phantom," the chiseled veteran began. "On the fourth flight of my second tour in Nam, I limped my jet back to the carrier. Although it wasn't the first time I'd brought one back all shot up, it was the first, and last, ejection I made." Tom's face sagged horridly as his mind reproduced a lifelike video of his experience.

183

"Approaching the carrier, the nose of the aircraft forcibly pitched down"—he used his hand to illustrate—"toward the water as I struggled to pull it back over the horizon. Fighting for control, I pulled the stick toward me as hard as I could. Initially, the Phantom pitched up erratically, and the G-force pushed me back into my seat, but then the bottom dropped out from underneath me as the plane stalled. It was as if someone grabbed the plane like a dart as it lingered vertically, then violently nosed it over, and fired it toward the ocean." His hand was still illustrating the Phantom's maneuver. "My head was driven into my chest, then thrown back against the seat. It was at that moment I knew I wasn't going to recover the jet, so my weapon systems operator—or wizzo as we call them—and I had to bail. I remember yelling, 'Eject! Eject! Eject!' as I frantically grabbed the ejection handle between my legs and initiated the sequence. A gunshot echoed between my ears as the canopy released into the atmosphere. Noise from the plane's engines whistled angrily, and a bang ignited rockets in the wizzo's chair, thrusting him into the sky behind me." He shot his hand toward the Piper Cherokee's roof. "Then it was my turn. Waiting for my seat to go, the seconds seemed like forever. My hands shook wildly, and my heart pounded so hard that it felt like it was going to jump out of my chest as I began to doubt the chair would even extract itself from the cockpit. Then it happened. A loud bang announced the unwanted amusement park experience I was about to encounter. Thrusting from the chair's rockets knocked the wind from my lungs and shoved me deep into the seat, as 3,000 pounds of force snapped my back like a twig." He placed his hand back on the yoke. "Strangely, I watched as the Phantom's red, hot exhaust flame plummeted away from me toward the Pacific. The clamor of noise gave way to the swish of my parachute deploying, then popping open overhead. I inhaled the warm salty air and checked my parachute, breathing a sigh of relief. That's the moment I realized I couldn't move my legs—the minute I knew my career in the navy was over—and that's how I wound up at Hines." Tom sat motionless, staring off toward the corona in the distance. The somber look on his face amplified his vacant gaze.

"What happened to the wizzo?"

"Huh?" Tom's mind snapped back into the present.

"The weapons guy?"

"Oh ... yeah, he was fine. No injuries." He shook his head and waved his hand. "Just me. So, what's the story with you? Why were you at Hines?" Tom quickly changed the subject. "Wait! I forgot. You're a doc. You must have spent time there practicing."

"Yeah, I spent time in Ward 1, but it wasn't as an intern or doctor."

Puzzled, Tom asked, "Then how'd you get there?"

"It's a long story."

"Yeah, but it's a long flight in a puddle jumper!" He checked his watch. "You have an hour and a half before our fuel stop, so you have time."

Conceding she began, "Well, the exemption may have thwarted Patrick's ability to enter World War II, but the discharge didn't extinguish his passion to serve. After the exemption occurred, false rumors circulated around town, alleging the only reason Patrick had received an exclusion was because my father, who was also a doctor and hospital administrator, gave him one. Some of that changed when we left Bemidji for Wichita, Kansas—"

"Kansas?"

"Yeah, defense industrial jobs—Rosie the Riveter ... Mike the Mechanic—we served too. Anyway, we moved to Wichita to escape a bunch of judgmental assholes and serve our country the only way we could."

"Sorry."

"You're forgiven," she joked. "Some of the scrutiny diminished when Patrick failed to return to the U of M for his sophomore year to ride out his football scholarship, but even today it still lingers around town like a wet, stinky, old fart—despite the fact my father wasn't even the guy who examined him!"

"Wet, stinky, old fart? I bet that left a stain?"

"Stick with me, Tom." Emma's humor lightened the mood.

Though the two had been at odds initially, the more they communicated, the more casual versus combative the conversation became.

"One afternoon while working at his father's gas station, Patrick caught an ad on the radio for Boeing and Swallow. Well, it was actually Boeing and Beech, but they were working through Swallow to recruit and train mechanics—"

"Sorry, still confused as to how you spent time at Hines."

"You said this was a long flight for a puddle jumper?"

"It is. How long is your story?"

"I don't know. I said it was 'a long story.' Maybe two or three hours?"

"The flight ain't that long!"

"Uh-ha ... well I'm getting there. Long story short,

though I put off medical school and followed him, I felt like I made the right decision in doing so. Shortly after arriving, we found a place to live. I was brought on to work in the blueprints room at Boeing, and he got an apprenticeship at Swallow/Beech"—her fingers made quotation marks— "as an aircraft mechanic."

"It was probably the greatest three years of my life, despite the war," she reminisced. "We got married and had great jobs. Patrick took flying lessons in his free time, and to top it all off, we both got to do something patriotic to help the war effort." Emma sat back in her seat as she relived those happy memories.

Even more perplexed, Tom chimed in, "It sounds like you had it all."

"We did until a telegram from Bemidji changed it all."

"How?" Tom's interest spiked.

"Jack Johnson, Patrick's closest friend, was killed in action while fighting in Italy." Her face drew a blank stare. "I knew him from my last year in high school up until he departed in January of '42 for the army."

"Sorry," Tom apologized.

"He was a great guy." She nodded, looking down at her feet. "I still miss his stupid jokes and the funny nicknames he'd give people. He always wore this annoying cologne that knocked the wind outta ya." Tears streamed from her eyes. "But it was like his signature, ya know?" She wiped her eyes before continuing.

"News of his death turned Patrick's world upside down. By that point, his waiver request had been denied, and now he was adamant he was going to join, no matter what they told him and even if he had to go to Canada."

Tom sat silently, making subtle altitude and heading

187

corrections while listening.

"The war was winding down but that didn't matter. We packed up everything and made our way back to Minnesota. He swore all the way back that he was going to 'walk right into that congressman's office,' with his rejection letter in hand, 'and demand an exemption.' And he did.

"Wow! He wanted to serve that bad, eh?"

"Oh yeah. You betcha." Emma nodded.

It took a year after his meeting with our congressional representative, but then it happened. I don't know how Patrick convinced them, but he received a waiver, so he enlisted in the Minnesota National Guard.

"Well, that's good. That's what he wanted."

"Yeah." Her head slightly rose. "After our meeting with the congressman in St. Paul, we drove to Bemidji. Patrick went to work with his father at the service station, and I went back to medical school at the U of M. The next four years went along pretty well. We purchased a home, and he bought a small Ercoupe that he would fly down to St. Paul so that he could visit me at school."

Tom was impressed. "The 415 was a great little plane for the money. Easy to fly and a breeze to land."

"Yep, it was a great little plane."

"What happened to it?"

"Korea." Another cryptic reference left her lips.

"OK, now you've given me two words—'Rucker' and 'Korea'!" Tom blurted out.

"I'm getting there!"

"I hope so. We have to land and refuel soon."

"I remember the day he left with his unit for Camp Rucker to attend training."

"Ah, Rucker!" Tom exclaimed.

"Although sub-zero temperatures chilled the station, Patrick set Great Northern Train Depot ablaze with his enthusiasm." Emma shivered at the thought of the freezing temperatures, which still felt so real that it made the hair on the back of her neck stand up.

"It was as though his exoneration was complete before any, and all, who had attempted to prosecute him in the court of public opinion regarding his exclusion from service." She sounded tough. "Regardless of the smiles and delightful expressions deposited on the faces of attending families, the truth was many didn't care for our boys departing for one war so soon after another had just ended." Her eyes scanned the darkness, speaking as though she were reliving the moment.

"Eighty-four enlisted. Five officers and one warrant officer, on the other hand, were exuberant, confident, and cocky."

"So he deployed?" Tom inquired again.

"Just hold on." Her index finger signaled a pause. "The men spent two days on a train, seventeen weeks going through basic training, and another eleven in advanced training—minus weekends and the fact that the families were able to join them once they graduated to advanced training. But the training and lack of a transition date to Korea began to wear on their psyche and spirit. That's when all hell broke loose."

"Well, there's going to be turmoil in a unit, especially one going to combat. That's just a fact," Tom pragmatically stated.

"Not this type of chaos." Emma's eyes met Tom's before she continued relaying the story...

RUCKER

Chapter Twenty-One

August 8, 1951—Fort Rucker, Alabama

"Emma, are you in there?" A man's voice probed loudly from the front of the elaborate two-story home. The shouting was accompanied by a frenzied rapping of knuckles on the weathered screen door. "Emma! Emma!"

Moving beside the house, Emma walked guardedly toward the front, where the man paced back and forth and hysterically called her name. Stopping short of the corner, she peered carefully around the home's wooden exterior to see who was yelling for her.

A few feet away, an army captain shadowed by two sergeants stood anxiously while they looked at the front door. Drenched in the hot, humid air of a sunny southern day, Emma stepped out from the building's short shadow into the harsh daylight to find a familiar face in Captain Hanscom.

"Scott, I'm over here!" she called out, drawing the soldiers' attention. Rushing to her side, Scott Hanscom could hardly contain himself.

Captain Scott Hanscom may have been short in stature, but he possessed a larger-than-life persona. A physician and colleague of Emma's, Scott had his own medical practice on the other side of Bemidji. Never competitive, the pair often acted as counsel to one another when drug or diagnosis questions arose.

Though he stood only at five foot seven, his square jaw, muscular arms, slick dark hair, and slate-blue eyes screamed athlete more than intellectual. Scott had joined the Minnesota National Guard in '49. Though their ages were separated by half a decade and they traveled in different crowds, parties and other gatherings often brought Patrick and Emma together with Scott and his wife, Sue. Like Patrick, Scott wanted to do something for his country. Though too young for WWII, he had joined right out of college with a desire to serve.

Her friend and colleague lightly grabbed her elbow. "I need you to come with me now!"

"Wait! Why?" Emma recoiled.

"I'll tell you in the jeep. Come on!"

"Scott! Carrie's on the back porch, napping. I can't just leave her."

"Crap!" He dropped his head, resting his hands on his hips. Within seconds, a few women and children from the neighborhood had started to gather, curious to find the source of the commotion.

"What's going on?"

"Emma, there's been an accident, and I need you to come with me." He looked directly into her eyes. "Do you have someone who can watch Carrie?"

"Yes, Maggie can." She pointed to her friend who had just arrived at her side.

191

"What's the matter?" Maggie broke in, concerned.

Hanscom's winded voice announced, "There's been an accident. I haven't got all the details"—his foot nervously tapped the ground— "but Patrick's been hurt, and I need you to come with me."

Emma's professional prowess quickly overcame her concern as a spouse, as the physician within took charge. "Maggie, would you—"

"Of course," Maggie cut her off without hesitation.

"Carrie is sleeping on the couch in the back porch." Her hand motioned toward the back of the home. "Let me grab my clutch, and I'll meet you at the jeep." She looked at Scott.

A cloudless sky freed the sun to beat down on Emma's face, causing sweat to bead on her upper lip. The stench of rotten eggs originating from the Bradford pear trees that invaded the Alabama landscape elicited a gasp from her as she rushed into the house to retrieve a small purse.

Emma and a number of other wives had followed the men to Camp Rucker, since families were allowed to join them once they completed advanced training. Patrick had rented an old mansion just north of the base in Ozark, Alabama. The rear of the structure had a beautiful screened-in porch, where the family spent the evening hours relaxing after Patrick returned from a long day of drill.

Emma wasn't fond of Alabama. She didn't care for the muggy subtropical climate, but most of all the multiple variations of venomous and non-venomous snakes. If not for the weekend trips they made to Panama City Beach in Florida, she would have abandoned Patrick after a month in the state. It wasn't until after a few startling events from the state's slithery vermin that she eventually learned how to coexist with the creatures.

Emma joined the men at an old Willys Jeep, where one of the sergeants assisted her into the rear of the vehicle. She sat beside Hanscom on a bench seat. As she adjusted herself, the sergeant abruptly sat in the passenger seat, while the other sergeant shifted the vehicle into gear and began driving.

"OK, I'm here. Now what's going on?"

"There was an explosion this morning while the men were practicing assault landings under simulated combat conditions on Lake Tholocco. Details are scarce, but it seems the landing craft that Patrick and some of the others were occupying was blown from the water after one of the charges simulating enemy fire exploded at the head of the boat."

"So where is Patrick?" Emma inquired with the professional tone of a doctor, unsure if he was dead or alive.

"He's at Ozark hospital with eleven others. I was told he broke his right leg and probably took a good jolt to the spine."

"What's the status on the others?"

"Most have broken limbs but I'm not sure." He shrugged. "I haven't been there yet. I received a call from Command, ordering me to retrieve you and get to the hospital as soon as possible. According to Colonel Swanson, all of the men were pulled from the water, but he wasn't sure if any had succumbed to the blast."

Watching city structures as they zoomed past, Emma caught the shimmer of a metal cross mounted on the apex of a church steeple in the distance. Silently she prayed for a miracle.

Rounding a corner into the hospital's parking lot, the jeep sped wildly toward the building. Stopping at the entrance, the sergeant who had assisted her into the jeep bailed out of the front passenger seat and helped Emma from the vehicle. Captain Hanscom followed, and they made their way inside. Pulling Emma to the side, he motioned for her to wait for a moment while he spoke with hospital staff. A moment later, he returned.

"May I see him?"

"Do you have your medical credentials with you?"

Surprised, she asked, "Yeah, why?"

"They said medical personnel only. Your credentials will probably get you back there."

"So his wife can't see him but a doctor can?" Emma exhaled angrily. "Since I'm a female physician from the North, I'm sure my credentials don't mean shit down here, but my relationship as his wife should," she countered, digging through her clutch for her credentials.

Since Hanscom had been so used to communicating with Emma as a fellow physician, the fact that Emma was Patrick's spouse had almost been lost on him.

A few minutes later, after Hanscom had spoken to the attending physician and presented Emma's credentials, he called her over. "Emma! Come on!" He motioned from a door that led to the back.

Cool white lights lit the passage, blinding Emma's eyes as the rays bounced off the walls and reflected off the floor. Swiftly they walked toward a room the medical staff had hastily transformed into a triage area so that they could contain the men arriving from the camp. Lysol disinfectant assaulted her senses, stinging the inside of her nose and making her eyes water.

Turning a corner into the room, she could see twelve men resting on beds made of silver steel tube, topped with thick mattresses and elevated so that the medical staff could easily attend to their needs. A few of the men were semiconscious, wading through a mental fog as they tried to regain their faculties, thanks to the pain medication each had been given. Those who were totally awake spoke softly with the military personnel and medical staff about their experiences.

Patrick was lying flat on a bed that was situated on the other end of the room. Emma could see the back of his head resting peacefully on top of a simple encased pillow. His arms were at his side, and his body was hidden beneath a pure-white hospital sheet, which cloaked any sign of injury he may have endured from the armpits down. As Emma approached, she noticed that his eyes and mouth were closed and his body was morbidly motionless. She prayed to see his chest rise and fall. Distressed by the lack of movement, she stopped at the end of the bed. Emma wiped away the tears that were welling in her eyes as she contemplated what she would do next. Lowering her hand, she was amazed when she saw his eyes flutter and face fluctuate a little.

Through the haze, Patrick was able to make out her figure. Prying open his eyes, he watched as Emma moved closer and hovered overhead.

"How ya doin, Killer Diller!" Emma quipped through her tears, trying to lighten the moment.

"I feel like I just got hit by a truck!" Patrick moaned, blinking erratically.

"Well it wasn't a truck"—she sniffled— "but from what Hanscom told me, it was quite explosive."

Rubbing his eyes, Patrick attempted to clear the cobwebs. "Shit, the last thing I remember was flying through the air!"

"All that matters is you're alive and still here with us," she commented, relieved to see him moving.

"What in the hell happened? Is anyone else hurt? Did everyone make it?" The questions rolled from his fatigued lips.

"From what I heard, yes! And from the way it looks, just lots of broken bones. As far as what happened, don't worry about that now as there are still a lot of questions. Just try and rest."

"OK." Patrick winced. The pain was intolerable.

"Do you need anything?" Emma asked as she leaned over him and touched his face.

"I'm just sore, Em. My leg and back hurt really bad." He gulped back a breath.

"You broke your leg. I'm sure they must've reset it. Your back is probably sore from the blow. I'm going to go over and talk to the attending physician. I want to see if there is anything more we can do for the pain. Try to rest."

Patrick swallowed, nodded slightly, then closed his eyes. Walking away from his side, Emma made her way past the other soldiers toward a tall, gray-bearded man with a serious look on his face. Motionless he stood studying one of the men's medical charts, his portly stomach protruding from a white exam coat that was at least one size too small for his current build. Though Emma appeared controlled on the outside, on the inside she was a chaotic bundle of conflicting thoughts and fears, deeply concerned about what the future would hold for the pair. She needed more information.

"Excuse me, sir. Can you tell me where the attending went?" she asked, searching the room for the man Captain Hanscom had spoken with to authorize her access to the room.

"Attending what?" The man cleared his throat, swallowed, and attempted to ignore her question, hoping she would go away.

"Physician." She tilted her head, tucked a loose lock of hair behind her right ear, and crossed her arms.

"I am the attending physician, Miss...?"

"It's Mrs... Mrs. McCarthy, and—" A distressed sound came from the man occupying the bed closest to her.

"OK, Mrs. McCarthy." His chin dropped toward his chest, further lowering his already droopy cheeks and allowing his eyes to peer over round wire-rimmed glasses that did nothing to enhance his pudgy bulldog-like face. "This is a hospital, not a kitchen. Is your husband one of these men?" He liberally waved around the clipboard that held the soldiers' medical charts.

"Well, yes, but—" Emma answered, angered by his assumption and flustered by his constant interruptions.

"Well, I can assure you, your husband is getting the best care we can provide, and you would do yourself good at home, tending to your children—more so than here." The chauvinistic windbag lectured her like a little girl, then rested the clipboard on her shoulder as he began herding her toward the door.

"I am—"

"I know, I know ... you are concerned about—" he began before Emma interrupted him.

"I am a physician!" Emma pushed the plump hand grasping the clipboard off her shoulder and raised her voice, determined not to be shut down by his arrogance. "And if you do not attend to the man whose chart you have in your hand this very second, he is going to drown in his own vomit!" she exclaimed, drawing his attention to a soldier reacting adversely to a shot of morphine the doctor had administered a few moments prior.

Dropping the paperwork to the floor in awe, the doctor rushed to the man, rolled him onto his side, and cleared his airway. After stabilizing the patient, he summoned a nurse a few beds away to tend to the soldier and monitor his progress. Gathering himself and the paperwork, the heavy-set practitioner retrieved a hankey from his coat pocket. Dabbing the sweat from his forehead and brow, he felt extremely embarrassed for not noticing the soldier's distress.

Facing Emma, he lost his imperious manner but avoided eye contact. "So, Doctor—"

"McCarthy." Her lips pursed and her eyes twinkled with a deep sense of satisfaction.

"McCarthy," he repeated. "How may I assist you?

Reveling in the moment, Emma could feel the stiffness in her lips morph into a grin. She knew she had the advantage now, and she was going to use it.

INDIGESTION
Chapter Twenty-Two

July 19, 1968–Somewhere over Kentucky

"Tom! Are you all right?" Emma watched as Tom smacked his chest with a clenched right fist, drumming up a belch.

"Yep, just indigestion from dinner." The pilot belched again discreetly. "So, how did life get more chaotic from that point? What exactly happened?"

Tom fiddled with the omni directional bearing selector to adjust the course line deviation between the aircraft's current position and the radial line that emitted from the VHF signal source, guiding the plane's direction.

Emma continued, "The men were simulating river crossings under fire. Following the incident, it was determined the boat Patrick and the others were using to make the crossing came into contact with a charge that was meant to simulate an assault on the landing party. Patrick was positioned at the bow when the boat was blown from beneath them. He received the brunt of the blast.

"After a few days at the hospital, it became obvious

something was seriously wrong with him. He continued to complain about his back. Although he could feel his legs, he couldn't move them, so Hanscom and I convinced the doctors to take an X-ray. The pictures identified broken lumbar and sacral vertebra."

Once again perplexed, Tom looked at her through what little light entered the cabin from the distant stars and half-lit moon in the sky, as well as the stray light coming from the gauges. Chicago's golden glow was well behind them, and only occasional yard lights that flickered intermittently below from the farmhouses provided depth to the aircraft's elevation.

"Sorry, Doc, I'm a pilot. I have no idea what part of my back was broken, so you have to give it to me in layman's terms."

"So in layman's terms, it's more commonly referred to as the lower part of your back and tailbone." Emma attempted to illustrate the region by pointing to her lower back.

Shifting back and forth in his seat, Tom seemed uncomfortable as Emma demonstrated how different regions of the spinal cord may be damaged and how each of those areas affect various parts of the body. Suddenly recognizing his agitation, and recalling a description of his experience expressed earlier, she cut short the narration.

"Sorry," Emma apologized. "I didn't mean to up—"

"No, no, don't be sorry. I was lucky." He rubbed his neck. "I can walk."

"Are you sure you're OK?" She probed, watching his fingers on his right hand massage the lower portion of his neck.

"Yeah, why?"

"It seems like something is bothering you."

"No. I just have to use the bathroom. You know us old farts." He chuckled. "We have about half an hour before our refuel stop then we will have two hours of flight time to Atlanta."

"Do you want me to continue? I really don't want to upset you." Emma gave him a concerned look.

"You can; I'm fine." Tom verified his altitude and heading, trying not to let her see his face as droplets of moisture gathered on his forehead.

Carefully she continued, "Within two days of receiving the results of the X-ray, the army decided Patrick needed to be transferred to Brooke Army Hospital in San Antonio, Texas. I packed up the house and made the thirteen-hour trip in our car from Ozark. The next several months were some of the most difficult I've ever experienced," Emma's sour voice conveyed while she gazed at a dull light gently reflecting off the polished silver yoke in front of her. "I went from wife, mother, and physician to nursemaid all in one day."

"You sound a little bitter. Your husband had just been through a life-altering experience," Tom vocalized, shifting awkwardly in his seat.

Emma stared at Tom. Dark shadows seemed to pool in her eye sockets, allowing her skeletal features to protrude sharply. The look she gave Tom made him reconsider how the incident had altered Emma's life, as well as Patrick's.

"After the army transferred Patrick to Brooke, his mother, Elma, came to Texas to watch over him, while Carrie and I traveled on the train to California."

"What was in California?" Tom asked, shifting even more erratically in his seat as he tried to get comfortable, but his back wouldn't allow him to do so.

Emma continued, "I decided it would be best to take Carrie to stay with my great aunt in Berkeley, California. She was single, loving, had a big house with a nice yard, and was really the only one available at the time who could care for her. "

"After a few weeks, I returned to San Antonio and found a room to rent. I drove to the hospital every morning and stayed until visiting hours were over, assisting the medical staff who were tending to Patrick, not to mention flipping the Stryker bed on the half hour."

"What's a Stryker bed?" Tom asked, feeling frustrated since he wasn't able to obtain relief from the uneasy feeling he had. He slid open a small window vent, allowing the atmosphere to cool his body. Though it was chilly, the perspiration still kept building up on the back of his neck and shirt. Countering the cold on his back, oven-hot heat blew in from the engine, baking his chest and further causing him to sweat. The two air masses collided, stabbing at his neck and arms, like lightning striking the earth in a violent storm.

"Do you remember a wedged bed with a silver stainless steel tube frame that turned horizontally, allowing nurses to roll guys with back injuries from back to front while keeping the spine immobilized?"

"Is that what they called that? I called it the 'roll and ralf'! Seemed like every time they turned me over on that thing I barfed!" Tom confided, the pain inside him residing a little.

"Anyway, after a few months, I could see the frustration and anger building in Patrick's eyes. I lobbied long and hard to get him into physical therapy, but the doctors at Brooke told him the only type of therapy he would benefit from was psychological, and they attempted to get me to convince him." Emma shook her head in disbelief.

"I had seen Patrick do phenomenal things in the time we were together, so I argued with them and got them to allow a transfer to the VA in Long Beach, California. The move at least allowed me to live and care for Carrie at my great-aunt's near Berkeley, then drive down and visit him on weekends. For six months, the VA in Long Beach attempted to help him with his recovery but failed to make any sort of progress toward the kind of results Patrick had hoped for..."

"Samuels Field traffic, Cherokee 1868 Kilo, 10 miles out landing runway 21, Samuels Field," Tom vocalized. After the call, he clicked the switch five times in succession, which made the amber lights lining the edges of the runway increase in brilliance, helping Tom to locate the field. Turning to Emma, he apologized. "Sorry. Had to announce our inbound position. We're gonna land soon, so when I make the next call, we'll have to go silent."

"No problem. So there was a belief among the doctors in Long Beach that Patrick should have been transferred to Vaughan General Hospital in Hines, Illinois, since the facility was better suited to care for the physical and psychological implications of his injury."

"That was the last place they should have sent him." Tom chuckled, still recalling his own experience while descending the craft, configuring the flaps, and slowing it for landing.

"We thought we were finally going to get the help we needed. So we packed up the car and drove to Illinois. We knew the hospital wouldn't allow Carrie in, so once again I had to leave her with my great-aunt in Berkeley. For six months, I busted my ass in Illinois, attempting to get him the assistance he needed, with little to no help from the VA. I finally got tired of doing nothing for myself and got a job at a small family practice nearby. That only made things worse, as it provided Patrick with free time to hang out with individuals he never would have in the past. It wasn't long before he became more concerned about where his next drink was coming from than his therapy.

"I complained about the amount of alcohol entering the hospital, but the more I complained, the more the staff dismissed it and stated it wasn't their job to babysit grown men. That was the final straw for me—"

"Just so you're aware, we're going to land in a few minutes. I'm going to make that five-mile out call I spoke of a few minutes ago," Tom interrupted.

"OK."

"Thought I would let you know. So you may want to wait and finish after we get back in the air."

"Are you sure you want to hear more?" Emma asked. "I'm sorry. I have just been sitting here, blabbering for the whole trip."

Now feeling a little better, Tom smiled. "Samuels Field traffic, Cherokee 1868 Kilo, 5-mile final landing runway 21, Samuels Field," he broadcasted once again before he said to Emma, "Well, you have blabbered on this long. I might as well get the rest of the story." Grinning, he throttled back the engine and fully lowered the flaps.

Stepping the plane down one hundred feet at a time, a green-and-white rotating beacon flashed in Emma's eyes as Tom crossed the threshold and course designation markings. He lowered the plane with a single bounce onto the touchdown portion of the runway, which was enhanced by painted pavement markings created for pilots to target during landing. After a short landing roll, Tom cleared the runway to the left, guiding the plane through the blackness of the night to the fuel pumps, by way of bluish-white lights identifying the taxiways.

Stopping the airplane in front of the fuel pumps, Tom completed his shut-down procedures, cut the engine, then set the parking brake. An irritating hum from the instrument and communications equipment followed a springy halt to the propeller's rotation. Turning off the master switch killed power flow to the devices and discontinued the drone. A loud noise followed in its wake, leaving a ringing sound in Emma's ears.

SMOKING

Chapter Twenty-Three

July 19, 1968—Bardstown, Kentucky

Lifting the handle, Emma popped open the thin metal door that divided the interior from the exterior of the plane, allowing tepid Kentucky air to drift into the cabin as the scent of charred oak from a local distillery ferried in. Inhaling the rich, scorched aroma, she quickly retrieved her heels, then grabbed the plane's roof and pulled herself from the seat. Exiting onto the wing and then to the tarmac, Tom followed her.

Arriving on solid ground, Tom stretched and waved his arms in the air, rolling his shoulders. Bringing his right hand to his left shoulder, he squeezed it sporadically. "I'm all bound up," he commented as he cracked his back and looked for base operations so that he could run in and use the bathroom. "I'll be right back," he told Emma before wandering past the front of the airplane and toward a brown brick building that was a few hundred yards away.

Emma watched Tom navigate the asphalt, still waving his arms and rubbing his shoulder. Watching him made her involuntarily stretch her back and arms, as though she were watching someone else yawn. Stooping over to stretch her back and touch her toes, she realized her feet were bare. Dropping the shoes next to her feet, she contemplated putting them on, then decided comfort, in this case, trumped fashion and picked them back up.

Wispy white clouds moved quickly through the moonlight overhead as she waited on the tarmac near the plane and studied her surroundings. A few feet off the passenger side of the wing stood two solid, white fuel pumps below an amber light, each tagged by reflective stickers containing the words "AVGAS 100LL" in white block letters on a royal-blue background. Lights from the airport's rotating beacon glinted off the metal signs, drawing Emma's attention to a warning placard that was stationed between the pumps. White block lettering on a fire-engine red background informed the flying public "No Smoking Within 50 Feet."

To her right lay a grassy area in the distance, just outside the pump's fifty-foot no smoking radius, which appeared to be the place to go for a smoke. Climbing back onto the wing, she kneeled just outside the door, stretched her arm into the cabin, dropped her shoes on the floor, and retrieved her clutch.

Returning from flight operations, Tom rounded the nose of the aircraft to see Emma's butt in the air and her head in the plane. Withdrawing from the interior of the plane, Emma turned to find him staring at her ass.

"Cigarette?" she asked, unsure of what to say.

Blushing, Tom's face turned almost as red as the background on the no smoking sign. She had busted him observing her curves and he knew it.

Coyly turning his glance toward the tail of the plane, he responded, "Sure ... yeah ... how about over here?" He pointed toward the grass. "That's out of the way."

Crawling down the wing backward, with her small bag in her grasp, she placed her feet down on the asphalt and stood upright, straightening her skirt. Turning, she followed Tom to the grass, then stopped a few feet away to remove a lighter and pack of Old Gold cigarettes from her purse.

Handing the container of butane to Tom, Emma withdrew two cigarettes from the foil pack, placing one in her mouth and ceding the other to him. Flicking the lighter, he lit her cigarette first then his own.

After lighting his cigarette, Tom returned the lighter and peered up into the sky. "There's a cold front swirling in from behind that will probably catch up to us near or over the Appalachians," he announced, exhaling smoke from his lungs.

"So?" Emma inhaled, gazing into the sky and noticing the clouds growing thicker overhead.

"Well, in pilot terms, that means we could run into some pretty good turbulence along the route. I just want you to be prepared for it." He took another drag from his cigarette, rubbing his shoulder again.

"Oh ... OK. Thanks." Emma chuckled. "In pilot terms," she repeated his reference and laughed. "Is your shoulder still bound up?"

"Yeah. Probably just hurts from that awesome carny ride the Phantom's seat gave me. The damn thing has hurt like this before."

For a few minutes, the pair stood silently, puffing on their cigarettes until Tom threw his butt to the ground.

"I suppose"—he stomped out the glow from his cigarette— "I had better refuel the bird." He headed toward the plane.

"Yeah, I suppose." Emma stomped out her own cigarette and followed him. "First I'm going to go in and use the bathroom!" she shouted. Holding his hand in the air, Tom acknowledged her and continued on to the gas pump.

With bare feet, Emma made her way to the building, stepping on a pebble here and there, which elicited verbal and facial responses from her as she cursed the jagged edges of the tiny pebbles poking her feet. Now almost totally overcast and cooling rapidly, the night air left tiny goosebumps on her exposed forearms, which refused to disappear despite her entry into the warm flight operations building, where the ladies' bathroom was.

Locking the stall door granted Emma a few minutes of privacy. Hiking up her skirt, she sat on the toilet, rubbing her arms and legs while she attempted to warm up. After finishing, she made her way to a small sink to wash her hands.

"No towels!" she wryly announced to herself, looking around the room. "Great!"

Shaking her hands rapidly in the air, she released as much of the water from her skin as possible before patting her hands dry on her dress. Gathering herself together, she checked her reflection in a large, rectangular mirror centered over the sink. Satisfied with her appearance, Emma strolled out of the bathroom, exiting the building and making her way across the tarmac, where the plane sat swaying in a northwesterly wind that seemed to have gained intensity since their arrival. Inside, Tom sat in the left seat, looking at a chart on his lap as he went over weather data. He held a flashlight in one hand and a pencil in the other.

"Hey!" Emma climbed into the right seat. "That wind is really picking up."

"Yeah, I want to get outta here and get above it." Tom grinned, then clicked on the master switch, allowing power to flow once again to the engine and instruments.

"How's your shoulder?"

"Ah ... OK. I have some serious heartburn though." He stowed the flashlight and pencil in a pocket, then placed his black headset back over his ears and smiled at her. Following his cue, Emma did the same.

"Are you up?" Tom asked, questioning if she could hear him.

"Yeah," Emma happily replied, clicking the intercom's rocker switch to talk.

After Tom turned the key, power flowed to the starter, rolling over the propeller and igniting the power plant. Releasing the brakes and increasing the throttle, he taxied to the hold short line, just prior to entering the runway. There he nosed the plane into the wind, set the brakes, and performed another run-up. Satisfied with the engine's operation, he made a radio call and announced his intention to enter the runway, then waited for an answer. As the field was not regulated by air traffic controllers, no one answered his call, so Tom checked the sky before taking the active runway, pushing the throttle forward to flood the motor with fuel.

Within seconds the craft was lumbering skyward. Following his instruments, he trimmed the plane through a layer of clouds, attempting a slower climb, then watched his direction-finding equipment, which would return the craft to its planned course. The propeller's pitch oscillated between high and low frequencies as pockets of turbulence made the plane ascend and descend in sync with the harmony.

Stuck in an unending soup of cloud-filled darkness, Emma fidgeted nervously, no longer able to see the lights from the ground. Unable to determine up from down, she could feel vertigo setting in, upsetting her stomach. Warmth flowing from the heat vent increased her distress, as she gripped the seat with one hand and her mouth with the other.

Noticing Emma's discomfort, Tom reached over and closed the vent, diverting hot air away from her. He began talking in an attempt to take her mind off the situation.

"So."

The intercom snapped to life in Emma's ears. "So, what?" Emma's scratchy voice filtered through the intercom as she took a deep breath of cool, rain-scented air, gulping back vomit as it attempted to make its way past her esophagus.

"The story. Are you going to continue?"

"Not sure I can without throwing up." She turned toward him in the darkness. A deathly pale color could be seen on her face through the dim lights, as the plane slammed and shook, blurring the gauges in front of her into squiggly lines. Her eyes struggled to keep up with the mayhem. Closing them tightly, she did her best to remove herself from the moment.

"The staff at Vaughan told you it wasn't their job to babysit grown men," Tom reminded her of where the story had left off. The turbulence to him wasn't anything he hadn't experienced in the past. Pulling what appeared to be a mint from his shirt pocket, he tossed it casually into his mouth.

Looking at Tom, Emma shook her head, releasing small bursts of vomit-laden odor into the air, which provided immediate relief to her sour stomach.

"Heartburn," Tom said.

"In the end, it came down to an ultimatum I gave him." Emma proceeded with her eyes closed and in a matter-of-fact tone, attempting to keep herself from puking by abbreviating the story. She breathed in the chilly, moist air. Raindrops gathered on the windscreen and began to streak over the glass, toward the plane's tail.

"I stated it's either me and Carrie or the booze! For a short time, things went well." She burped. "We left Hines and headed for California. There we stayed at my great-aunt's in Berkeley for a couple of weeks until we concluded Bemidji was where we needed to be so that he could run his parents' service station, and I could return to my practice." She was interrupted by a loud banging sound coming from the plane. Ignoring it, she continued, "At the time, that made the most sense.

"After arriving in Bemidji, I soon discovered that weeks of sobriety had become a myth once he cavorted with old buddies and began drinking exorbitantly. At first, he attempted to hide his drinking from me but I knew." The bumps and bangs of the aircraft jumping through the atmosphere almost seemed to disappear as she looked to the back of the plane.

"You stated earlier that I sounded bitter. I don't believe it's bitterness so much as disappointment. I expected more out of him, not just for me but for our daughter as well. If

I am bitter about anything, it's about the way I was treated, as his alcoholism magnified his rage, which was often unloaded onto me." Somberly she exhaled.

"What did he do?" Tom queried, now a bit nauseous himself.

Emma stared blankly at the blurred windscreen. Lightning bolts periodically flew across the sky in front of the plane, overruling the darkness and blinding her with brilliant bursts of silvery-white light. A bang close to the plane startled her. The storm's assault on the exterior of the small aircraft rattled her, compelling her to tighten her jaw and clench her fists. Rain exploded off the structure's surfaces, and thunder grumbled through the cabin, suffocating the propeller's buzz. An electrical burst through the intercom was followed by a crackle, which sent shockwaves to her core and traumatically transported her back in time.

BIRCH LANE

Chapter Twenty-Four

———◆———

August 12, 1958—Bemidji, Minnesota

Closing the front door to the small two-story home, Emma collapsed a long, clear bubble umbrella and then removed her knee-length trench coat. Exhaling the cool, moist air blowing in off the lake, by way of a late summer storm, she attempted to catch her breath after her short run up the front walk. But suddenly her lungs were violently attacked as they became overcome by smoke from a cigarette that was smoldering slowly beside numerous half-crushed butts in a glass ashtray, which sat on the edge of an oak end table. The smoke drifted effortlessly into the air, lingering ghostlike in the amber light of the table lamp that stood next to the ashtray. The cigarette's asphalt odor mingled with a woodsy, whiskey barrel scent, slightly camouflaging the putrid smell of puke and piss.

The sight of Patrick lying unconscious on a fabric-worn couch, as Carrie roamed unsupervised about the home, infuriated Emma. A bottle of Jack Daniels that held about a quarter of the caramel-colored whiskey sat by his feet.

"He had one job!" Emma thought, disgusted by the sight of bile-yellow puke running down the front of his white variegated polo shirt. Vomit had spattered and dried over various shades of narrow brown stripes running vertically down the shirt. The repulsive scent of his urine-soaked khakis nauseated her as she approached the couch and stood over him in disbelief.

For over a year, Emma had catered to his liquor-induced belligerence and self-pity, believing sympathetic commiseration and compassionate empowerment would spur him to want more for himself and his family than the angry, broken, paralyzed, alcoholic burden he'd allowed himself to evolve into.

Patrick's neck angled sharply to the rear of the davenport, and his head rested against the top of the sofa. His arms dangled limply beside him, and his paralyzed legs were sprawled out in front of him on the floor. As Emma stood over him, water from her umbrella and coat, which she was still holding, dripped onto the intricate hardwood floor. Patrick released a loud snort from his mouth that jarred his head, almost waking him from his alcohol-induced slumber.

Emma no longer had the time or the wherewithal to put up with his self-pity. Between the hospital visits and the hours, days, and years that had been spent by his side as she assisted him with his recovery, she'd gone above and beyond her duties as a wife. It was all now coming to a head, while she thought about what she would say or do next. Then it occurred to her that the time for talking was over.

Pummeling Patrick relentlessly over his head and chest with her parasol, Emma gave him a murderous look, which caused her complexion to crease in angry frown lines and wrinkles.

"You damn son-of-a-bitch, lazy lowlife, piece of motherfucking shit, stupid lying asshole! I can't stand you! I can't stand what you've done to us! I can't stand who you've become and what you've reduced us to. I can't stand what you've done to our daughter. I've busted my ass for you—cared for you when you couldn't care for yourself. Loved you when you didn't love yourself, and you threw it all away! Emma screamed at the top of her lungs without taking a breath while ruthlessly beating him over the head and chest.

Her anger flowed freely until Patrick woke up and grabbed the makeshift weapon. With his head throbbing and chest pounding, confusion set in as he clutched the pointy end of the umbrella. Emma's voice quivered, and she shook hysterically, though she still gripped the handle tightly. Tugging the aluminum shaft, she fell into his lap. Patrick seized her wrist and ripped the umbrella from her hands, throwing it to the floor. Stunned, he wrapped his left arm around Emma, pinning her to his chest, as she twisted and flailed wildly, trying to escape.

"Let me go! You son of a bitch! Let me go!" she yelled, spearing her petite elbows into his chest and kicking him violently. "I hate you! I fucking hate you!" All sense of elegance left Emma, as the exhausted woman cussed like a sailor.

"Stop it!" Patrick yelled, embracing Emma's rib cage so tightly that it felt like it could pop. Liquor-laden sweat percolated from his oily glands, further sickening Emma and polluting her airspace. "Stop it! Stop it, you little bitch!" he slurred.

216

"Little bitch?" Emma sharply questioned, her pale skin turning a deep red as her struggle continued.

Frantically she fought, jolting violently until a silver flash of chrome caught the corner of her eye. The burst of light, followed by the sound of a pistol's spring system actuating the hammer, brought her fight to a halt. In his right hand, Patrick held a cocked and loaded snub-nosed 38 caliber revolver to the side of her head.

"Settle down!" he barked ferociously.

"Oh, you son of a bitch! Do it! Come on, do it!" Emma cried, daring him to pull the trigger. "I've had it! Do it!" she screamed, breathing heavily. "Do it! I don't want you anymore. I don't want us anymore. I don't want to live like this anymore!"

"I'm going to, you little whore!" Patrick raged, pushing the end of the barrel against her temple.

"What happened to you? What happened to us? You used to love us! Now all you love is liquor!" she railed against him. Intentionally pushing her head against the barrel's opening, she sobbed uncontrollably. "Do it! Come on!" she screamed.

"My life is shit!" he hollered.

"Your life is shit? What about mine?"

"Maybe if you weren't out whoring with Hanscom!"

"Whoring? I'm out making a living! Trying to keep what's left of my career intact but it's impossible here, especially when no one wants to come to my practice because my husband is the town drunk, and I can't fix him, so how am I gonna fix anyone else?" Emma wailed, breaking free from her captor.

Gasping for air, she stood facing him, realizing if he was going to shoot, he would have already. Though the revolver was still aimed at her, there was no way he was going to discharge it. "If it weren't for Hanscom ordering the X-ray, you would've laid in Ozark for another month while the idiots there tried to figure out what was wrong with you! If it weren't for me, you would still be stuck in that piece of shit VA hospital in Hines!" Emma screamed, throwing her hands in the air, then walked over and retrieved the empty bottle laying by Patrick's feet.

"Jack was killed in the war; no one can change that." Emma pointed the bottle at him. "If you want to join him, go ahead." She waved the bottle carelessly about. "But I refuse to stick around any longer and watch you destroy yourself and our family!"

Across the room, a noise alerted Emma to a pair of ice-blue eyes peering at them beneath a head of long copper-red hair.

"Mom?" Eleven-year-old Carrie called out from around the corner. The argument had drawn her to the end of the hall, where she stood trying to comprehend the commotion.

Turning toward her daughter, Emma reassured her, "Mommy will be right there, honey. Go to your room." Following her mother's instruction, the young girl disappeared from sight.

"You can shoot me with that gun, or you can shoot yourself. I really don't give a shit! I'm done!" Her muscles tightened as she spoke defiantly to the man she'd grown to hate. Tossing the bottle to his lap, she surrendered. "I can't take it any longer! I'm done." She shook her head as tears streamed steadily down her cheeks, dropping onto her coat. Sniffling, she added, "Carrie and I will be at my father's house. You can stop by and see her there, if you'd like."

Silence took hold of the room as Emma walked away from the living room to pack and prepare Carrie for the journey ahead of them. The gun, still in Patrick's grip, lay sideways in his lap while he stared blankly into space.

Exiting the home, Emma held a suitcase in one hand and Carrie by the other as they walked to the car. Never once looking back, she lifted her chin boldly into the cool breeze and guided Carrie through the drizzle to the old Chrysler Airflow, which was parked on the street. Half of her heart loved him, but the other half loved herself more. Though the thunder and lightning had subsided on the inside, the rain was still falling gently outside. Emma opened the front passenger side door and assisted Carrie into the vehicle. She then moved to the door trailing, opened it, and loaded the suitcase into the back seat. Closing the metal door, water droplets streaked down the car's jet-black exterior and dripped onto the flooded street. Moving purposely around the back, Emma opened the driver's side door and got in. Pausing for a moment, she focused on the rain-soaked windshield in front of her. She became enchanted in the serenity of the silvery droplets sliding down the slope. Glancing over at Carrie, Emma smiled gently, turning the key in the ignition, as it brought the car's engine to life. Shifting the car into drive, she checked her field of vision for other vehicles, then pulled away from the curb. Lightning struck the surface in the distance, while the main body of the storm waned behind them. A light grumble from a distant charge passing through the atmosphere rumbled through the Chrysler, agitating Carrie.

"Don't worry," Emma touched her hand to soothe her. "There will be lots of storms in your lifetime, but don't let them scare you."

THE STORM

Chapter Twenty-Five

July 19, 1968—Somewhere over Tennessee

Emma continued relaying the story to Tom. "Carrie and I stayed at my dad's place for a few months until I decided what to do next." Absorbed by the thought of Patrick holding a gun to her head, she attempted to distract herself from the image. Outside the plane, the storm had relented a little, allowing Emma to relax her grip on the seat.

Unsure of what to say, Tom sat silently as the propeller droned on. Occasionally the stillness was interrupted by their headsets crackling from the electrically-charged atmosphere. The aircraft had settled into smoother air after passing the weather front but was still bouncing a bit through pockets of rough air.

"Eventually Carrie and I found a place, then relocated to Eagle Lake. I opened my own medical practice and put my life back together. Patrick and I never divorced. Why? I don't know." She shrugged. "I made a half-assed attempt to get along with him after he moved to St. Paul. His cousin offered him an opportunity to work on his political staff if he quit drinking. For the most part, he straightened himself out, though not totally. It quickly became apparent his addictions had morphed from just alcohol to women."

"Sounds like your estranged husband's a real winner," Tom noted, once more becoming uncomfortable in his seat.

Laughing out loud, Emma answered, "Yeah."

"Occasionally he would come and stay at the house. I allowed it because he traveled so much with his hectic schedule, and sometimes it was the only way he could spend time with Carrie. But his partying and womanizing also drew media attention. After Patrick made a few visits to my place, the reporters began trolling the shoreline of the lake where I live in an attempt to get pictures or a reaction from me."

"Why?" Tom asked.

"They knew we hadn't divorced and thought I would comment on his antics." She laughed. "I never did though. I'd just wave and continue with what I was doing. It happened so often that I began referring to their harassment as 'magical McCarthy moments'."

"Eventually Carrie went off to school and followed in her father's footsteps. No matter what that man did, she always found a reason to blame me for the relationship's failure," Emma reflected as the airplane began to encounter again a substantial amount of turbulence.

"I don't know why, but a part of me always wanted him to come back. Hell, I still love the man," she admitted just before the aircraft banged violently, coming into contact with another hostile pocket of air.

Peering at his instrument panel, Tom guided the plane through a starless black sky. The cloudy stew obscured any light from above or below, leaving Emma off balance and dizzy. For a moment, she felt as though she were spinning, but her mind convinced her it was only her imagination.

The seriousness of the situation hadn't occurred to her until Tom ceased communicating as frequently as he had been and instead began paying more attention to the gauges.

A wild rollercoaster feeling overcame her as the plane dropped and slammed.

"Wow, that was one helluva bump!" she yelped.

Calmly, Tom answered, "Yeah, flying over the mountains can be tricky."

"How far out are we?"

"About an hour," he estimated, holding the yoke steady while fighting a feeling of instability, both from the plane and inside his body. An uncomfortable pain followed by a dull, crushing discomfort in the center of his chest made him gasp. Within seconds Emma could see through the instrument's low light that something was happening by the look on Tom's face. His breathing became shallow, and a faint wheezing sound leaked from his airway. Suddenly his arms drooped, and his body slumped back in the chair.

"Tom! Tom!" Emma yelled, grabbing the yoke.

Emma struggled to control the aircraft as it jolted from one rough pocket of air to another. Hurriedly she scanned her memory for anything she could recall from her days of flying with Patrick that could help her. She pushed the talk button on the yoke.

"Help! Can anyone hear me?" she yelled frantically into the boom mic.

Over the radio, the broken sound of a man's voice calmly answered her distress call. "Aircraft calling for help. Please identify."

"Ah ... yeah ... my name is Emma and I need help!"

"OK, what's the problem?" The controller patiently sought information.

Distraught and winded, Emma spoke without pause. "The pilot is unconscious. I think he had a heart attack. We're on our way to Atlanta and I need help!"

"OK. Emma is it?"

"Yes."

"Have you flown before, Emma?" The man asked, hopeful that he could talk her through landing the plane even with minimal flight time.

"Flown, yes. Piloted an airplane, no!" Emma's terse voice answered as she struggled to keep the plane straight and level.

"OK, first thing I need you to do is tell me what kind of plane you are in."

Other controllers could be heard, providing direction to pilots in the background.

"Small, one engine. Comanche, I think. I'm not sure. I'm really getting thrown around."

"On the front panel, do you see a box with four knobs sitting directly below white-colored numbers?"

She leaned forward, searching for a box fitting the description. While leaning forward, the yoke slid toward the nose of the airplane, placing the small airframe into a gradual descent.

"Found it!" her transmission roared back. "It says KT76TSO!"

"That's it! I need you to turn each one of the knobs until the fourth number reads 7-7-0-0."

Unsure of what she was doing, Emma turned each

small black knob until the box read 7-7-0-0. Raising her head, she found it increasingly difficult to sit back in her seat. The feeling made her pull back on the yoke, then forward again, making the plane porpoise, like a whale swimming through the ocean, until she realized the yoke only needed to travel a short distance back and forth to make the airplane climb or descend.

"OK!" she shouted.

"Push the little button next to the word "ident." That way I can see you."

"There's a little black button on the box. Is that it?"

"Yes!"

"OK." Emma reached forward and pressed the tiny button.

Waiting patiently for a response, the controller clicked his mic. "Good! I have you." His voice sounded relieved.

Not receiving another communication from him for what she believed to be minutes, but in actuality was only seconds, Emma became increasingly agitated and nervous. A moment later the radio sprang to life again.

"Ma'am, I need you to push the throttle forward and gently pull the yoke back a bit. It looks like you have lost a lot of altitude and you are way lower than you should be according to what the pilot filed on his flight plan. Do you know how to do that?"

"I hate it when they call me ma'am!" She said to herself and shook her head. "I'm not sure. How do I control the throttle?"

"It's in the center of the console. There's a black T-shaped lever. I need you to push it forward as far as it will go."

"I'm not sure which one it is! The plane is shaking violently!"

Emma panicked and began clicking the mic switch hysterically.

Concerned, the controller stood up at his console as though he were going to jump into the pilot seat and fly for her. He raised his voice instead. "OK, stick with me. It's a black T-handle, just above your left knee sticking out near a red star-like knob! It protrudes toward you, and should be below the center of the instrument panel."

"No! No, I don't see it! Just get me down!" she screamed.

"I will, but right now I need you to add power! You are going to stall the plane if you do not add power. If you don't find the throttle, lift the nose, and climb, you are not going to make it over the mountains. Did you find the throttle?"

"I don't want to make it over the mountains! I want to land!" Stricken with fear, she grabbed the yoke and pulled it toward her, fighting the controls that had become sluggish as the plane began to stall. Pushing the mic switch again, she cried out, "I can't see anything outside! I want to land. Please let me land! I want to land!"

Pressure from wind striking a small tab on the underside of the wing activated the stall warning horn in the cockpit, as the airplane pitched up without warning and began to buffet from side to side. Blaring rambunctiously, the noise from the horn wailed through the cabin, adding to Emma's agony.

The mic remained keyed as Emma shrieked, "The plane is shaking! Get me down!" Her voice and words were high-pitched and unhinged, deafening the controller, as screams of absolute terror filled the headset covering his ears.

Watching the radar scope, the man concentrated on the blip as it continued to move, losing speed, but gaining altitude. "Push in the throttle! Push the yoke forward!" he yelled, demanding compliance.

"Oh my God! I'm tipping back! I'm tipping back! Oh my God!"

"Emma!" he radioed, not knowing what to say.

"Tom! Wake up! Wake up! Tom!" she screamed over the mic. "No! No! No!" Her voice raucously shrieked over the air as the plane stalled, nosed over, and sped toward the ground.

Inaudible words and unrecognizable sounds accosted the controller's ears. "Emma, push the nose over and increase the power!" he waited for a response, searching for a blip on the scope. Only the crackle of static answered his call, and the small, round green light once vibrantly flickering on the black background ceased to exist. The controller's face drooped as his skin became ashen, and he fell into his chair, defeated.

"Emma, talk to me!" He made one last call, hoping for a response. Tears filled his eyes while he pulled the communications equipment from his head and dropped it to the floor. Placing his head in his hands, he prayed...

ILLUMINATION

Chapter Twenty-Six

July 20, 1968—Georgia Baptist Hospital

On the day following the assassination attempt, Carrie arrived early at the hospital. Stepping into her father's room, she abruptly stopped, surprised not only to see him sitting slightly erect underneath sanitary, white hospital sheets, but also laughing heartily in the company of a thirty-something-year-old woman. Though she was relieved to see that he was no longer at death's door, she couldn't help but be irritated that he was in the company of a strange woman.

Beside Patrick's bed, an exquisitely dressed woman sat next to him, gushing over him like a groupie meeting Paul McCartney for the first time. She giggled a bit too childlike for her age. Gently stroking Patrick's hand as though she were brushing a poodle, it was obvious to Carrie the woman was more interested in her father for reasons she hypothesized to be less than wholesome.

Stopping just short of entering the room, Carrie stood steely, with her arms crossed and head lowered, in judgment over the scene. Carrie's fashion style gave her an affluent, youthful appearance. She wore a broadcloth shirt with small, brown embroidered flowers, which blossomed against the top's white background. Her culottes were an identical color to the embroidered flowers on the shirt, and a slim, brown leather belt with a gold buckle circled her waist. On her feet, she wore brown leather St. Trope slingbacks with a one-inch block heel. Two cut-out flowers, staggering in height and size, decorated the square toes of her shoes. A brief glimpse at her attire would lead one to assume that Carrie was a pleasant and cheery person, but a look at her expression and body language could quickly change that original assessment.

"Good morning, Father!" She pursed her plump, red lips and flared one of her crimson brows as she stared jealously at the scene of her dad slobbering all over the lavish woman.

"Good morning, doll!" Patrick apprehensively swung his head away from the attractive brunette to look at his daughter, offering a broad smile.

"You're alive. And even sitting up a bit." Carrie was thoroughly amazed to see him so bright and lively, only hours after the event.

"Yeah, why wouldn't I be?" Patrick searched her eyes, confused. "Would you have rather seen me dead?" He chuckled peculiarly, then turned his gaze back to the dark-haired woman.

"Ah ... well ... you took two bullets to the gut. I pretty much had you for dead yesterday. Just impressed you're even alive." She moved toward the foot of the bed. "When I left here late last night, they'd moved you from surgery to the recovery room, but they weren't sure if you were going to make it, or even how long it would be until you woke up if you did." Carrie straightened one of the sheets that had been indiscriminately tossed over his paralyzed legs, as she made her way to her father's side.

"Yeah ... well ... thank God I'm not dead!" Doc said there was a lot of blood loss that they were worried about even though the bullets missed major organs," he commented but didn't turn his gaze away from the woman who had fully captivated his attention.

"You're just a lucky guy, I guess," Carrie declared sarcastically, her cheeks turning a brighter shade of red than her hair. She was astonished the woman sitting across the bed from her was visibly unimpressed with Carrie's sour character. Folding her arms combatively once more, Carrie waited a few minutes for Patrick to introduce his friend. Lowering her gaze, she turned back toward the foot of the hospital bed and marched slowly in a goose step, clicking her heels all the way to the bed's corner. Then she twisted swiftly, eyeing the skinny Sophia Loren look-alike. She just knew this woman was more than a mere acquaintance of her father's.

In a haughty tone, she interrogated the woman. "Since my father isn't going to do it, I will. I'm Carrie McCarthy. Who are you?"

Standing pensively, the bodacious, jet-black brunette extended her hand. "Barbara ... Barbara Cray. It's a pleasure to—"

"Barbara here is an old friend from St. Paul," Patrick interrupted to beef up what he believed Carrie would accept as a logical justification of his acquaintance with the younger woman.

229

"Old friend, huh?" Carrie smirked smartly, staring at the warm hand that had been presented but refusing to offer her own in return. "She's what? Half your age?" She shrugged, sizing up the condition of Barbara's skin, the barely noticeable lines in her face, and the gray, knee-length sheath dress that was tailored to her hourglass curves. "Nice dress. I'm surprised a woman with your figure isn't sporting more of a drop skirt style," Carried added, implying her body was a tad bit too large for the dress she had on.

"Well, aren't you a dear?" Barbara said in jest, dropping her hand but refusing to abandon eye contact with Carrie. "I should get going, Pat. You need your rest, and I have to check in at the motel." She smirked, turning her back to Carrie as she retreated to the chair she'd occupied in order to retrieve her purse and luggage. Balancing herself on the chair's seat, she stooped and gathered her belongings.

"Staying long, are you?" Carrie sneered, arms still crossed over her chest.

Barbara stood upright as she placed her purse strap over her shoulder and then brushed lint from her dress with her hand. "As long as it takes," she scoffed, authoritatively cocking her head.

Turning toward Patrick, Carrie broiled with anger. Her head swooned and her heart sank. Suddenly she felt sick to her stomach and fatigued, but most of all disappointed in herself for years of deliberately averting her eyes from his blatant infidelity. In an instant, she understood all of her mother's anger, criticism, and animosity. Sullen, her head dropped and she felt sorry for her mother and all that she'd put her through over the years. Her epiphany spurred a resolution to rejuvenate their relationship.

"Mother is on her way here right now. Her plane should have landed earlier this morning. I called her when we thought there was a possibility that you weren't going to make it." Turning back to Barbara, she said, "So ... Barb. I think we can handle *Pat* on our own." Carrie's tone was snotty and bitchy as she mocked Barbara for abbreviating her father's name.

"I've heard a lot about you, Carrie." The more experienced woman took a few steps toward the callow girl and stopped. "I hope all of the rumors I've heard aren't true," she looked Carrie up and down, her demeanor poised and unflinching.

The rhythmic footfall of wooden shoes echoed down the hallway becoming louder as they approached then paused in the doorway to Patrick's room interrupting the sudden cold and uncomfortable silence that had settled between the ladies.

A cocky smile flickered on Carrie's lips as she turned toward the door.

"It's about time you got he—" She abruptly blurted, then stopped at the sight of a legislative aide entering the room.

"Sir, there's someone here to see you."

THE END

ACKNOWLEDGMENTS

Beverley Bertholf and Roland Gary —my grandparents— *Tholocco's Wake* could never have been created without your story.

My wife **Leanne**. Always the optimist, she said "you can" even when I thought "I couldn't". Over the years, she has stood by me through some of the best and worst moments and enriched my life with her steadfast love.

I must also thank **Catherine Kennedy Plasschaert**, Delta Airlines Captain and friend from the days I spent as a cadet with Civil Air Patrol. I was grateful for the opportunity to reconnect with her after years of pursuing different paths through life. The aviation portions of the novel would not have been as accurate without her help and expertise.

Rosanna Chiofalo Aponte, my editor, is an award-winning author and has been a consummate mentor. Thank you for helping me dig deeper, and convey the story within the story from the train wreck draft manuscript I handed you.

To the folks at **Atmosphere Press** who assisted me in bringing this book to life.

ABOUT ATMOSPHERE PRESS

Atmosphere Press is an independent, full-service publisher for excellent books in all genres and for all audiences. Learn more about what we do at atmospherepress.com.

We encourage you to check out some of Atmosphere's latest releases, which are available at Amazon.com and via order from your local bookstore:

Fire, A Girl, and Far Too Many Aliens, a novel by Ava Woodhams

Yellow on Blonde, a novel by Stephen M. King

A Gathering of Broken Mirrors: Memories of New York Survivors, a novel by Anthony E. Shaw

Dragon Stones: A Soran Drayce Novel, by Amy Henriod

Ghosts of the Abbey, a novel by Ashley Wellman and Patrick Kinkade

And Still We Rise: A Novel about the Genocide in Bosnia, by Jordan Steven Sher

The Prisoner and The Executioner, a novel by Catee Ryan

The Special Case of Hazel Louise, a novel by Amanda Culaccino

ABOUT THE AUTHOR

Warren W. VanOverbeke enjoys the serenity of walking Lake Michigan's shoreline with his wife Leanne when not writing historical fiction.

Born and raised in Minnesota, he attended Hill-Murray High School then went on to Cardinal Stritch University, the American Military University, and Michigan State University, attaining degrees in Business, International Relations, and Equine Management.

He is a United States Air Force Veteran, and wounded warrior from the war in Afghanistan.

Warren lives in Benona Township, Michigan, where you may find him either repairing fences his horses have decimated or chasing his granddaughter who runs with scissors.